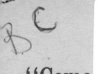

"Come

"I want that kiss you promised me so long ago! The one that I was too weak and hungry to survive," Lincoln added, holding out his arms.

"Is that reasonable?" Cassie asked, feeling a great surge of longing to be in Lincoln's arms.

"Perfectly," Lincoln replied. "I want you to know that you can trust me at all times."

"But you still have that cast on," she whispered hoarsely, setting down her glass and moving closer.

"It wouldn't stop me," he said, softly. "Nothing would, except my desire to do nothing that you wouldn't want me to." His eyes glowed with a luminous warmth that destroyed the last vestige of Cassie's resistance.

Katherine Arthur is full of life. She describes herself as a writer, research associate (she works with her husband, a research professor in experimental psychology), farmer, housewife, proud mother of five and a grandmother to boot. The family is definitely full of overachievers. But what she finds most interesting is the diversity of occupations the children have chosen—sports medicine, computers, finance and neuroscience (pioneering brain tissue transplants), to name a few. Why, the possibilities for story ideas are practically limitless.

Books by Katherine Arthur

HARLEQUIN ROMANCE

2755—CINDERELLA WIFE
2821—ROAD TO LOVE
2905—FORECAST OF LOVE
2948—SEND ME NO FLOWERS
2971—REMEMBER IN JAMAICA
2991—THROUGH EYES OF LOVE
3014—LOVING DECEIVER
3043—MOUNTAIN LOVESONG
3061—ONE MORE SECRET
3103—TO TAME A COWBOY

Don't miss any of our special offers. Write to us at the following address for information on our newest releases.

Harlequin Reader Service
P.O. Box 1397, Buffalo, NY 14240
Canadian address: P.O. Box 603,
Fort Erie, Ont. L2A 5X3

NEVER DOUBT
MY LOVE

Katherine Arthur xx

Harlequin Books

TORONTO • NEW YORK • LONDON
AMSTERDAM • PARIS • SYDNEY • HAMBURG
STOCKHOLM • ATHENS • TOKYO • MILAN

Original hardcover edition published in 1990
by Mills & Boon Limited

ISBN 0-373-03146-7

Harlequin Romance first edition September 1991

NEVER DOUBT MY LOVE

CHAPTER ONE

'I AM in love with Lincoln Snow. I shall love him forever.'

Cassie Lewis smiled to herself at the entry in her old diary. August the tenth, of the year she was fourteen. She flipped through a few more pages. On September the first the entry read, 'I saw Lincoln Snow today and he smiled at me. I almost fainted.' It might have been only puppy love, but nothing else Cassie could remember had ever felt quite so wonderful. Unless it was the soft, cuddly warmth of the puppy that Lincoln had brought her on the day after her dog, Monty, was killed on the road that ran between the Snow estate, Oak Hill, and the Lewis farm. Dear old Monty II. He still patrolled the Lewis farm, a little arthritic now, but devoted to the family with every fibre of his lovable being.

Lincoln Snow had found Cassandra huddled miserably by the roadside with the huge, limp body of the first Monty in her arms, sobbing her eyes out. He had held her close and murmured soft, comforting words in her ear, and when she'd looked at him she had seen that there were tears in his eyes and his cheeks were wet. It was the first time she had seen a man cry, and it had startled her. Her father was a stern man who seldom showed strong emotions of grief or joy. Lincoln, she had learned, could not only cry, but the next day had laughed joyously when she'd hugged him to thank him for the new puppy. He was so very happy, he had said, to have made her feel better.

'That settles it,' Cassie said aloud, after recalling that remark. Lincoln was in need of a nurse now, someone to make *him* feel better. She had not really planned to take on another private duty job right away, if ever, but, if Lincoln Snow would have her, she would take the job. She tucked the old diary back into the box of mementoes from home that she always carried with her, and went to her telephone. Lying beside the phone was the notepad on which she had written the New York number that her mother had given her from the Midvale Press advertisement. For Lincoln Snow was returning to Oak Hill to convalesce from a tragic fall which had almost cost him his life, and he needed a nurse.

'He fell from his penthouse terrace and went through a skylight below,' her mother had told her. 'Didn't you read about it in the papers?'

'Mrs Sedgewick doesn't leave me much time to read the papers,' Cassie had replied. 'Poor Lincoln. That sounds terrible. But I don't know . . . I'll have to think about it. I'm about ready for a break.' Recently, Cassie had found herself wondering if she wasn't going to be ready for nursing care herself by the time she could turn Millicent Sedgewick over to a practical nurse. The elderly lady hated television and insisted that Cassie play hearts or gin rummy with her during almost every waking moment when Cassie wasn't tending to her other needs. It seemed to buoy the old lady's spirits to be able to trounce Cassie at cards, but Cassie was ready to scream at the sight of a deck. Still, if Lincoln Snow needed her, she could gather her frayed nerves together and pitch in.

'Mr Snow's residence,' a rather high-pitched voice with a very British accent answered Cassie's call.

'Willton, is that you?' Cassandra blurted, surprised. The Snow's butler had looked ancient the last time she saw him, over ten years ago.

'Yes, madam. To whom do I have the pleasure of speaking?'

'Cassie Lewis,' she replied, suppressing a giggle at the extreme formality of his answer. 'And it's still "Miss". Do you remember me?'

'My goodness, yes, Miss Cassandra!' he said, and Cassie could picture the way the old man's thin face crinkled into a smile like a parchment wrinkling on familiar creases. Willton had always seemed to like her. Perhaps, she thought, out of sympathy for her dislike of Lincoln's nephew, Tyler Spenser, a whiny, mean, spoiled brat of a child who had become one of the Snows' brood when Lincoln's older sister and her husband had been killed in an accident. Cassie still remembered how she had caught Willton smiling benevolently the time she'd pushed Tyler into the Oak Hill pond during one of the elaborate Easter egg hunts that Lincoln's mother gave for her own younger children and all of the children in the neighbourhood. Willton had looked quickly away and regained his usual severe demeanour, but ever after he had seen to it that Cassie had extra cake and ice-cream whenever she was invited to Oak Hill.

'It's very good to hear from you,' Willton went on, after taking a second or two to recover from his surprise. 'Did you call to enquire after Mr Snow?'

'Partly that,' Cassie replied. 'I heard about Mr Snow's accident, and my mother called to tell me he'll be needing a nurse when he returns to Oak Hill soon.

I'm an RN now, and I'm just completing a private duty job in Chicago. I'd like to apply for the position if it's still open. I can send Mr Snow my references, if he'd like to look them over.'

There was a short silence, and then Willton said with what, for him, was remarkable enthusiasm, 'Miss Cassandra, the job is yours. Mr Snow is... that is, he's put me in charge of filling the position, and I think you'll be just what the doctor ordered. A familiar face, you know, at a time like this, can mean a great deal. I can't tell you how pleased I am to find that you're a nurse. How long have you been in that profession?'

'About four years,' Cassie replied. 'I came to Chicago for nursing school and I've been here most of the time since, but it will be wonderful to go home again. Tell me, how is Mr Snow getting along and exactly when is it you'll need me? Do you know yet? I can't recall when it was the accident happened.'

There was a longer silence this time. 'It's been a month, and Mr Snow is not responding as well as we'd hoped,' Willton finally replied carefully. 'That's the reason that I... that is, Mr Snow's doctors and I... decided that removing him to his old home might be beneficial. He can be moved as soon as the house is opened and special transport can be arranged. I'll let the medical people tell you the details of his condition when you meet them. I know there are multiple fractures and a great many stitches and other injuries. They appear to be healing properly, but Mr Snow's spirits are not coming around. It's... very worrying, Miss Cassandra. Very worrying, indeed.'

'I can imagine so,' Cassie replied, frowning to herself. 'Do you have any idea what the problem is?'

'Nothing but personal speculations,' the old man replied, sighing. 'I don't believe it would be proper for me to comment along those lines. But perhaps, once you've talked to Mr Snow...'

'Of course,' Cassie said quickly. Ever proper Willton was not going to give her a run-down on Lincoln Snow's private life, but, if she found out something and wanted to ask him specific questions, he would answer.

They conversed for a little while longer, concluding with Willton's promise to notify Cassie as soon as he knew when they would be needing her. Along the way, Cassie found out that Lincoln had a four-year-old, slightly handicapped daughter who would be coming with them, accompanied by her nanny. There was no mention of the child's mother, so Cassie assumed there must have been a divorce. She had only vague recollections of hearing that Lincoln had married. It must have happened after she recovered from her own infatuation with him, she thought, or else she would have had a tear-soaked page in her diary. Even now, she found that she was rather pleased to find that there was not a wife in the picture.

'Shame on you, Cassandra,' she told herself. What if the missing Mrs Snow was the key to Lincoln's depression? What if his fall hadn't been an accident at all? Cassie shuddered and shook her head. She had better stop imagining things and wait and find out the truth from Lincoln. Right now, she would call her family and tell them the good news. She was coming home to stay with them for at least a few days until she would be going to live at Oak Hill for as long as Lincoln Snow needed her. Which, she figured, shouldn't be more than a couple of months at most.

It was now the first of March. That should give her plenty of time to get involved in the new Shakespeare Festival at Midvale College this summer. After that, she'd decide if she wanted to keep on nursing, or try for a full-time career in the theatre.

For some time, Cassie had felt that nursing was probably not her true calling. More than once during her training she had got in hot water for talking back to a doctor whose demands she'd thought unreasonable. Working in the emergency-room of a big-city hospital had not brought out the best in her either. One night the emergency-room team had managed to breathe life back into a young man who had had far too much to drink and then wrapped his motorcycle around a telephone pole. When, his sobbing mother at his side, the boy had been wheeled off to Intensive Care, the doctor had called her aside, his face livid with anger.

'Miss Lewis,' he'd snarled, 'your remark to that poor woman was inexcusable. How dare you suggest that it might have been more helpful if she'd been at that boy's side earlier? How do you know she wasn't? Have you no sympathy? No pity?'

Cassie had been so upset by what she had just witnessed that she had snarled right back. 'Doctor, after working here, my heart bleeds for the whole human race. But just last week that sweet little mother was in emergency with a drug overdose!'

'And you think it's going to help her to snap at her?' the doctor had said sarcastically.

'No, but I don't think buckets of sympathy are going to help either,' Cassie had replied, suddenly aware that she was in trouble and had better moderate her tones. 'I wish I knew what would. I could make millions.'

'Then perhaps, until you receive the revelation, you had better keep your mouth shut if you want to continue your training,' the doctor had said icily, then turned on his heel and walked away.

Cassie had managed, with difficulty, to do so, but she never was able to look upon a mangled body as simply a machine that was broken, as some of her colleagues claimed they did. She felt very strong emotions, more often anger and frustration than sorrow, it seemed. 'How could you do this to yourself?' she wanted to cry. Where was that wretched, sobbing family before this happened? Why didn't anyone care until it was too late?

There were, of course, many cases where no one knew what had happened, or where the victim was clearly not at fault. Cassie still hated it, especially the night shift. She was so drained by the morning that she felt like an automaton.

'Marry me,' had suggested Kevin Mayfield, the young intern she had been dating for several months, when she'd complained. 'As soon as I finish up, you can stay home, join the country club, and take up golf.'

'Thanks, but I'd hate that even more,' Cassie had replied. 'I've got to have a career. It's just that I sometimes wonder if nursing is it. I wanted to do something to help people, but most of the time I feel like I'm trying to stop a haemorrhage with a . . . a postage stamp.'

'You're just tired,' Kevin had said sympathetically. 'We all get that way. Why don't you go home and get a good day's sleep, then come with me to dinner and the theatre? My brother's repertory company is out at North Park this week and next, and I've got free tickets whenever I want to go.'

'Your brother's? I didn't know he was an actor. Or is he in the business end of things?'

'No, he's an actor. One of the leads.' Kevin had looked quite proud. 'One of the New York critics called him the best young Shakespearian actor in the country.'

'That is impressive,' Cassie had agreed. 'All right, I'll go. What are they performing tonight?'

Kevin had consulted a schedule he pulled from his pocket. 'Tonight's *Othello*,' he'd said, 'and Martin's doing Iago.' He looked at Cassie and grinned. 'After seeing him in that, you'll swear you couldn't trust him with your back turned, but he's really a great guy. You do like *Othello*, don't you?'

'Oh, yes,' Cassie had said quickly. 'It's one of my favourites.' Actually, she had only a vague, general idea of the story. She had better see if she couldn't find a copy somewhere before tonight, so she wouldn't appear too stupid! Fortunately, Cassie's roommate had had a one-volume edition of the works of Shakespeare, and when she'd awoken later that day she'd gone over the play. She had been looking forward to the evening with great anticipation when she had finished, for it was going to be interesting to see if the brother of easygoing Kevin Mayfield could convince her that he was the most evil of Shakespeare's villians.

By the time the play was over, Cassie had been entranced as she had never been before. Not only was Martin Mayfield superb, but the whole experience had set something inside her on fire. What might it be like to be on that stage, bringing one of Shakespeare's great stories to life with such force that it made a movie or television production seem, at least to her, like a poor imitation? When, afterwards, Cassie had asked Martin that same question, he'd smiled knowingly.

'There's nothing like the theatre. If you can feel it like that, you should try it. You're much too pretty to be emptying bedpans. We settle in for the summer in Connecticut, and there are apprenticeships you can get by trying out. Why don't you? You can always go back to being a nurse if you don't make it.'

'Oh, I couldn't,' Cassie had said modestly, but his words had started a seed growing which had persisted until the next year when she had been to graduate from nursing school in the spring. She could at least attend the try-outs the group held while they were in Chicago. If she succeeded, she could take the summer off, then go into private duty nursing, an option she had decided might suit her better than a hospital environment.

Cassie had succeeded, thereafter spending the next three summers with the Shakespearian company, and earning professional status as an actress, but always going back to nursing when there were no jobs available that paid an adequate salary. She had still had her student loans to pay off, and had not been able to afford the luxury of taking a low-paying job. Finally, after her stint with Millicent Sedgewick, she would be debt-free. Like a sign from the heavens, Cassie thought, had been the announcement she had seen only yesterday in the *Theatre News* that a Shakespeare Festival was going to be held for the first time that summer at Midvale College, directed by

Ogden Warren, a friend of Cassie's older brother, now
the head of the drama department at Midvale. They
would hire some professionals, and use some student
actors.

After completing her conversation with Willton,
Cassie sat for several minutes staring into space.
Should she call Ogden now or wait until she got to
Midvale and go and see him? Competition for those
professional jobs would be fierce. She glanced at her
watch. He might be home from his office by now. She
had his number. Seconds later, the phone at Ogden
Warren's home was ringing.

'Warren here,' answered an almost British-sounding
voice.

'Cassie Lewis here,' Cassie replied. 'Ogden, you
sound very British these days.'

'Cassie! Of all people! I was just talking to Martin
Mayfield about you this afternoon. He called after
he saw our notice in the *News*. Can I dare to hope
that you've decided to abandon your Florence
Nightingale fixation and come and join us?'

For a moment, Cassie was not sure that she had
heard Ogden right. He hoped she was coming to join
them? Sending silent thanks in the direction of Martin
Mayfield, she replied, 'I certainly would like to. Tell
me all about it.'

That invitation brought on such a lengthy, minute
description of everything involved in the new
Shakespeare effort that Cassie was almost glad to hear
Mrs Sedgewick ringing her bell vigorously.

'Duty calls, Ogden,' she said. 'I'll come in and see
you the first chance I get when I'm back in Midvale.'

'Do that,' Ogden agreed. 'I'll have you read for Kate in *The Taming of the Shrew*. I'm not above a little typecasting.'

'Typecasting! Of all the nerve!' Cassie exclaimed. 'I'm just a sweet little saviour of the sick and suffering these days. But I can *act* the part of a shrew.'

'Hah! "'Twas told me you were rough, and coy, and sullen",' Ogden quoted. 'Or was the man a rejected suitor, perchance?'

'Perchance,' Cassie replied. ''Bye, Ogden.' She was not going to discuss her love-life with Ogden Warren, who had always been as gossipy as a whole women's bridge club rolled into one. The fact that she had come close to saying 'yes' to proposals from each of the charming Mayfield brothers would certainly give Ogden grist for his gossip mill. She could imagine him saying, 'Have you heard about Cassie Lewis? She not only can't decide whether to be a nurse or an actress, but she can't decide whether to marry a doctor or an actor. Do you suppose it's one of those multiple personality things?'

'Goodbye, Cassie love,' Ogden said, snickering as if he had already thought up something juicy to pass on. 'Don't take too long bashing poor old Lincoln Snow into shape.'

He hung up before Cassie could retort that he was going to be the one that got bashed if he started calling her 'love'. It was bad enough to put up with that phoney accent from someone she used to watch catching frogs along the Oak River, without his getting stagey with her too.

Cassie hurried off to take part in her employer's bedtime ritual game of hearts, for once soundly beating the elderly woman.

'Are you sure you haven't been letting me win all along?' Millicent asked suspiciously.

'Not a chance,' Cassie replied. 'I play for keeps. I think today is my lucky day.'

Her mother also commented on Cassie's good fortune when Cassie finally called her late that evening.

'I think Lincoln Snow and Ogden Warren are the lucky ones,' her father, on the other line, said gruffly.

'Why, thank you, Dad,' Cassie said, feeling a warm glow at her father's compliment. He dealt them out sparingly, but, when he did, she knew they came from the heart.

Cassie lay awake far into the night. Was it, she wondered, the excitement of realising that she was really going to do some leading roles in Shakespearian productions in the coming summer, or was it the fact that she was actually going to be living with and helping Lincoln Snow? She hoped she could help him. She could not imagine that beautiful smile of his turned cold and bitter. But there had been something vulnerable about him, the man who wept with her for her lost dog. If something or someone had hurt him deeply, it was going to take a lot more than a new puppy to make him feel better again.

'I'm frankly at a loss as to what might bring him around,' the doctor told Cassie only a week later when she met him before going to see Lincoln for the first time. 'He refuses to talk or to eat, even though he could be taking some liquids by mouth now. You'll see that he's still on maintenance IVs. We can't take the chance of his getting run-down while his body is trying to repair all of the damage.'

All of the damage, Cassie soon learned, sounded more like the inventory of a whole hospital than one patient. A skull fracture, over a hundred stitches in his face alone. 'The fracture's healing well. No brain damage. He was lucky it was apparently a glancing blow the way he hit, or else...' The doctor gave Cassie a meaningful look and went on, 'Most of the facial scars can be surgically removed, once he's well enough.' In addition, the doctor detailed broken ribs, fractures of both the right radius and ulna, a compound fracture of the right femur, some mild internal injuries, multiple contusions. 'Very fortunately,' the doctor concluded, 'there was no severe injury to his back. It seems Mr Snow had the presence of mind to tuck himself into a ball and take most of the blow with his right shoulder and arm.'

'That doesn't sound like anything he can't recover from completely fairly fast, if he wants to,' Cassie said.

'It certainly isn't,' the doctor agreed. 'Oh, one other thing. He refuses anything but ibuprofen for the pain. That's the only thing that's called forth any remarks from him at all, and those were very—er—graphic. He seems to want to suffer.'

'Then he can't be resting very well,' Cassie commented. 'I'll see what I can do.'

'Good luck,' the doctor said, but his expression was not encouraging. 'Do you want me to come in with you?'

'No, I'd better see what kind of rapport I can establish alone,' Cassie said.

The doctor nodded. 'You know where to reach me if there's any change, and I'll stop by this evening. I must say, I'm relieved to leave him in such capable

and familiar hands. Someone who hadn't known
Lincoln might be intimidated by this formidable
house. This is the first time I've ever been in this place.
It reminds me of some baronial estate on the
continent.'

'I've heard that Lincoln's great-grandfather was
trying his best to intimidate the whole county,' Cassie
said with a smile, 'but his parents weren't like that at
all. They had a big, rollicking family, and really liked
children. I didn't know Lincoln all that well because
he was one of the oldest, but, when any of the younger
Snow kids had a party, all of us in the vicinity were
invited. I'll try bringing back some pleasant memories. Maybe that will help.'

Cassie said goodbye to the doctor, then took a deep
breath and walked briskly to the door of the adjoining room and opened it.

It was a large, beautiful room, with high ceilings
and tall windows, which overlooked the pond and the
meadow beyond. White curtains hung at the airy
windows, and on the walls a richly coloured floral
design hinted at the kind of furniture the room usually
held. All that remained of that furniture was a massive
dark armoire. Everything else had apparently been
removed in favour of white, utilitarian hospital fur-
nishings, more easily kept clean. Even the heavy rugs,
which doubtless should have been on the floor, were
gone, leaving bare the parqueted oak.

Cassie crossed silently to the hospital bed, where
Lincoln Snow lay on his back with his eyes closed,
an IV quietly dripping its life-giving fluid into his left
arm. When she looked down at him, she felt the
saddest ache she could ever remember place its ten-
tacles around her heart. His face, his handsome,

ruddy, smiling face, was pale and criss-crossed with scars. Thank heaven, she thought, that his eyes were spared. If he had not had fairly prominent brow ridges, they might not have been. His soft brown hair, doubtless shaved off a little over a month ago, was growing back, but it looked dull and lifeless.

Fighting a strong and unprofessional urge to lean down and put her arms around him, which would probably only cause him more pain, Cassie instead took hold of Lincoln's left hand and held his cool fingers in her warm hands. He made no response. It was impossible to tell whether he was awake or asleep.

'It's Cassie Lewis, your new nurse,' she said softly, bending over him. 'Do you remember me?'

Lincoln Snow's eyes opened slowly. He looked at her, his hazel eyes surprisingly clear and direct. He made no reply. A few seconds later he closed his eyes again and turned his head away.

Cassie continued to stand there, holding his hand in hers, tears coming to her eyes and trickling unchecked down her cheeks. 'Worrying,' Willton had said. This was far beyond worrying! She gave Lincoln's hand a little squeeze, then blindly retrieved the clipboard of charts from the end of his bed and made her way to a chair. She sat down, the clipboard on her lap, then suddenly bent double, trying her best to stifle the sound of her sobs. If it had almost destroyed her trying to take care of victims whom she did not know, this was going to finish the job. How could she cope with it?

While visions of the Lincoln Snow she had once known, healthy and handsome and happy, clashed in her mind with pictures of the sadly damaged man who lay just across the room, she fought back her tears, raised her head and wiped her eyes. She would cope because she had to. She was not going to let this happen to Lincoln Snow! She was going to see to it that he got better, in all ways, no matter what it might take to do it!

CHAPTER TWO

CASSIE meticulously went through the mass of records, taking note of the comments of other nurses and making herself a careful schedule of what had to be done and when. For the next couple of days, she decided, she would simply go through the procedures and watch Lincoln, talking to him a little as she went along, trying to evaluate what his responses were, trying to pick up any clues as to what was keeping him so deeply depressed. She wanted to be able to reach him emotionally, somehow, but did not want to cause him any undue physical pain by getting him upset more than necessary. But, if it took getting him upset to get him to talk to her, she would do that as a last resort. Hopefully, that would not be necessary.

With that decision made, Cassie returned to Lincoln's bedside. 'Time for the eternal thermometer,' she said. There had been a note that he sometimes refused to co-operate by opening his mouth, and she thought that she saw his jaw tighten a little. Instead of trying to force that issue, she quietly pulled down his covers and tucked the thermometer under his left arm. At that, he opened his eyes and looked at her. She smiled. 'I saw you clamping your jaw shut.' While she held the thermometer in place with one hand, she gently caressed his shoulder with the other. 'I may as well tell you,' she went on, 'that, once I'm familiar with the way your skin temperature feels, I can tell what your temperature is within a few tenths of a degree, so that it won't contribute anything to your attempts to be uncooperative to not let me take your temperature. Of course, if you just want to annoy me, go ahead and try. I have the patience of a saint.'

Cassie could not tell if her remarks had had any effect, for Lincoln again closed his eyes. Which, she thought, was probably just as well. She was doubtless looking slightly guilty at telling such whopping lies. She might be able to guess his temperature within a degree or so, but no one on earth had ever accused her of having a saintly temperament.

Once the temperature was recorded and the small, disposable implement tossed away, Cassie began a careful inspection of her patient from head to toe. She tried to think of him as just another person in a hospital bed, but failed so completely that she gave the cause up before she had finished looking over the scars on his face. Every scar touched her as if it were etched on her heart. She found herself once again fighting back tears, telling herself over and over that she must control her emotions. It was perfectly all right to feel more involved than normal, she told herself, and to communicate that to Lincoln with her gentle hands. That was, after all, one of the reasons that she was here, instead of someone else. And the reason she had to stay.

So, as she inspected the stitches and clamps that remained in his scalp, she gently caressed his head, and felt his ears and neck with soothing strokes of her hands. Above the wrappings on his ribs, a patch of chest hair was regrowing, curly and dark reddish-brown. Something about it reminded Cassie of seeing Lincoln as a young boy, when she was quite small, bare-chested and long-legged, swinging from a vine by the river and then dropping into a pool with a Tarzan-like whoop.

'Tarzan's grown some hair on his chest,' she remarked, smoothing her fingers across it, a tingle running through her own hands at its crisply sensual feeling. 'Did they always choose bare-chested men for that role?' she mused aloud to keep herself from thinking too much about her own response. 'I can't remember any with hairy chests.'

Next, she uncovered his long, hairy legs, the right one still in a heavy cast. 'I'll be glad when that's out of the way,' she said. 'It's no fun turning someone with one of those on.' Very slowly she felt the musculature from his left thigh to his ankle, squeezing and massaging as she went. 'Need to get those muscles back in shape,' she commented as she reached his toes and gave them a friendly tweak. 'You'll need them to walk with crutches pretty soon.' After that, she carefully bent his left leg at the knee and applied a little pressure against his foot to see if he would offer any resistance. 'I'm glad your back wasn't severely injured,' she said, 'otherwise I couldn't do this.'

At first, Lincoln's leg moved only when she moved it, a heavy, limp limb that seemed almost detached from a human body. But, after she had bent and straightened it by her own force several times, Lincoln let her bend it again, and then pushed it straight quite forcefully, almost putting Cassie off balance. For a second, she almost told him that if he did that again he'd pay for it later, but she managed to keep her thoughts to herself.

'Very good,' she said instead. 'Let's do that again.'

But this time, Lincoln held his leg straight, refusing to bend it. Cassie chuckled and leaned against it for a moment. 'That's good too. Either way will help.' She let go, catching a brief flicker of something in the eyes that Lincoln again opened and fixed on her for a moment. Was it anger? she wondered. She would be glad even for that, as long as she did not provoke him so much that he sent her away.

'Blood-pressure next,' she said, taking the sleeve and wrapping it around his arm. She put her stethoscope in her ears and pumped the pressure up, then listened intently to the steady, strong pulsing of Lincoln's blood. He might be trying to knock on death's door but, deep inside, his own body was contradicting his wishes with a good reserve of vitality. His blood-pressure had been running low, but the reading that Cassie got was well within the normal limits. Was it something that she had done? she wondered. She wrote the numbers down, saying as she did so, 'If you ever want to know what I'm writing down, just ask. It's no secret.' She bent over Lincoln so that if he opened his eyes he could not avoid looking into hers. 'Now,' she said, 'I am going to take a break and have a cup of coffee. When I come back, I'm going to give you a bath and shave you. Don't go away. I give lovely baths.'

As Cassie had hoped, Lincoln did open his eyes for long enough for her to smile at him and wink. Before he could close them again, she wheeled swiftly and left the room.

Good lord, she thought, consulting her watch as she hurried down the elegant staircase to the first floor of the huge mansion. It was almost ten o'clock, still early in the day, but she felt as if she had been at work for an entire shift. She was going to have to take some extra vitamins to keep up with this kind of emotional drainage. Right now, however, she wanted to see if she could find Willton and persuade him to talk to her while she had her coffee. She needed to have a little more information on Lincoln Snow's recent past to guide her.

She had just reached the bottom of the stairs when she heard Willton's distinctive voice coming from the huge salon, which was just now being got back into liveable-in condition after being wrapped in dust covers since Lincoln's parents had moved to Florida to escape the midwestern winters.

'When I say clean, I mean down into every little crevice,' he was instructing a young woman, who clutched a bottle of cleaning spray in one hand and a cloth in the other and stared apprehensively at a huge brass gargoyle sitting on a pedestal. He looked up at the sound of Cassie, clearing her throat to warn of her approach. 'Ah, good morning, Miss Cassandra,' he said. 'Is there something I can do for you? Have you a report on our patient?'

Cassie nodded. 'If you don't mind, Willton, I need to talk to you,' she said.

Willton immediately looked anxious. 'Carry on,' he said, waving his hand in the direction of the cleaning woman and hurrying to Cassie's side. 'Not worse, I hope,' he said in a low voice.

'Not at all,' she replied softly. 'Physically, Mr Snow is doing quite well. But, if you'd come with me while I have some coffee, I'd like to ask you some questions. I hope you realise that, as a professional, I will hold anything you tell me in strictest confidence.' She hoped that telling Willton that would encourage him to abandon, at least partially, his own conscientious protection of Lincoln's private affairs.

'I'll tell you what I can,' Willton replied. 'Shall we go into the morning-room? I'll bring the coffee myself. We don't have the staff as well organised as they will be in a few more days.'

In the hexagonal room on the east end of the mansion, the lower part of one of the towers that gave an almost fairy-tale aura to the place, Cassie sat at a recently polished table while Willton went into the kitchen, returning with a small electric coffee-pot and two cups. 'Things aren't quite right yet,' he apologised again. 'This is hardly the proper coffee-service for the occasion.' He poured them each a cup of coffee, as elegantly as if it were a silver service, then sat down opposite Cassie. 'What is it that I can tell you, Miss Cassandra?' he asked. 'Did Mr Snow say something that aroused your curiosity?'

'No, Willton, he still isn't talking,' Cassie replied. 'However, I don't believe that he's suffering from a true depression, in spite of what the others have said. I believe that he is very unhappy over something and thinks that he doesn't want to get better. From what I remember from my psychiatric nursing courses, that is quite a different thing, and not nearly as threatening a situation. However, I still need time to be sure, and some information so that I don't blunder on to the wrong topic and make him feel even worse. You must realise that I don't know much about what's happened to Mr Snow in the past ten years or so. I didn't even realise that he had married and had a daughter until just recently. Does the fact that his daughter is here with her nanny mean that Mr Snow and his wife are divorced? Is there some trauma connected with their life together that I should know about?'

'Oh, no, Miss Cassandra,' Willton said quickly. 'Mrs Snow died when Colleen was born. It was a premature delivery, brought on by a fall that Mrs Snow took. Miss Colleen is four years old now. She has cerebral palsy, but it's not severe. She has learned to walk with a brace on one leg, and her speech is somewhat impaired but seems to be improving a little lately. She's a very bright child.'

Cassie studied Willton thoughtfully. He was still not telling her anything except bare facts, and she was not entirely sure that he wasn't keeping something from her. He had said, 'Oh, no,' almost too quickly. She might as well plunge into the realm of emotions and see what she could find out. 'How did Mrs Snow's death affect Lincoln, emotionally?' she asked. 'What I want to know is, were they very close? Did he mourn for a very long time?'

Willton looked uncomfortable. 'I wouldn't say that they were close,' he replied, 'although Mr Snow was a very devoted husband. Mrs Snow—her name was Magda—was very headstrong and discontented. She was not...' Willton paused and cleared his throat. 'She was not the person I would have chosen as a wife for Mr Snow.'

'I see.' Cassie tried to think her way through the fog of propriety that Willton sent up. Magda Snow had obviously not been one of his favourite people. She and Lincoln had not been close. Lincoln had been devoted, but apparently not Magda. Put that together with the fact that she was discontented and it might imply that she had some extramarital escapades of which the observant Willton was aware, but not

Lincoln. Now there remained the child of this imperfect union. 'How did Lincoln get along with Colleen before the accident?' she asked next. 'Did they spend a lot of time together?'

'I wouldn't say a lot,' Willton replied carefully. 'Of course, he's been a very busy man, and he did stop in the nursery every day, but he has not been what one would call a devoted father, which has been rather a puzzle to me.'

'Why is that?' Cassie asked quickly.

'Well, when the little tyke was first born,' Willton replied, 'Mr Snow stayed at the hospital day and night, and when she was first brought home he used to spend a great deal of time holding her and rocking her in his arms. But, a few months later, he suddenly spent much less time with her. I'm not sure whether it was related to the discovery of her handicap or not. Not that she has ever wanted for the very best of care, but I would have thought that he would...' Willton stopped, frowning. 'It's just not what I would have expected of Mr Snow,' he concluded finally. 'Not what I would have expected at all.'

Cassie reached over and patted the old man's thin hand. 'I understand,' she said. 'Lincoln has always been so warm-hearted and sympathetic. He brought me a puppy once, you know, when my old dog was killed. But, when a parent finds out that his child is handicapped, it's not unusual. They feel guilty and unhappy about it, and don't know what to do. With cerebral palsy, there's really nothing much to do, except help the child do the best they can with what God gave them. It's hard to accept. Very hard.'

Willton pursed his purplish lips together. 'I believe that's probably Mr Snow's difficulty,' he said at last.

'He does tend to take on the weight of the world at times. But I don't believe that would be the reason he is so unhappy now.'

'Do you have any idea——?' Cassie began, but she was interrupted by another woman, this one a rotund person wearing an apron.

'Mr Willton,' the woman said, 'I beg your pardon for interrupting, but if someone doesn't get me some potatoes there isn't going to be any dinner tonight. If someone would just tell me how I could get to town...'

'Mrs Comstock!' Willton said severely. 'I am never to be interrupted when I am talking to Miss Lewis! Never! Do you understand?'

'Y-yes, sir,' Mrs Comstock replied, visibly shaken. 'I'm sorry, sir.'

When she had left, Cassie smiled at Willton. 'I can see that you have your hands full trying to get this place running again, and I'd better get back to Mr Snow. Why don't you go ahead and save Mrs Comstock from a nervous breakdown? You've given me a lot to think about, and we can talk some more later. At least I have an idea what the problem is *not*, now.'

'I'll be glad to help all I can,' Willton said fervently. 'I'll try to think of anything that might help you.' He stood up, then paused. 'You probably weren't aware that Mr Tyler has been Mr Snow's ward for the past several years,' he said.

'Tyler? That little monster?' Cassie blurted.

'Yes, Miss Cassandra,' Willton replied, looking disgusted. 'The same one. Mr Snow's parents were unable to handle him, and so Mr Snow took over for them. He's been living with Mr Snow since he was fifteen. For about five years.'

'No, I certainly didn't know that,' Cassie said.
'Where is he now? Did he stay in New York?'

'I don't know where he is, Miss Cassandra,' Willton
replied stiffly. 'I haven't seen him since Mr Snow's
accident.'

That was interesting, Cassie thought, as Willton
drifted off to deal with Mrs Comstock and she climbed
the stairs back to Lincoln's room. At least two of the
members of Lincoln's recent household were people
whom Willton was not very fond of. Poor old fellow.
It was hard enough to run a perfect household in an
imperfect world, without having to put up with other
constant irritants. Funny that Tyler would have dis-
appeared after the accident. But then, Cassie had
always had the impression that Tyler would rather not
deal with anything unpleasant. If things weren't just
the way he wanted them, he would whine and complain until someone gave in just to shut him up. She
couldn't blame Lincoln's parents for having wanted
to get rid of him. How they could have stood him
until he was fifteen, she couldn't imagine. They
probably kept hoping for some miracle to turn their
grandson into someone as nice and well-behaved as
their own flock. Cassie could have told them that
would never happen after her own experiences with
him. Tyler was as cruel as he was disagreeable. But
why on earth would Lincoln take him in? The only
place for Tyler Spenser would have been a strict mili-
tary school, preferably somewhere in Siberia. Cassie
sighed and shook her head. She knew the answer to
that. Gentle, soft-hearted Lincoln probably hoped he
could succeed where his parents had failed.

Cassie opened Lincoln's door very softly and peeped inside. His head was turned and he was gazing speculatively at his IV bottle.

'It's about time to change that, isn't it?' she said, making her presence known as she walked to his bedside. 'I'll disconnect you while you have your bath, and then hook up the newest version. I think it's chocolate fudge with cherries floating in it.'

This time, Cassie was definitely aware of a flash of anger in Lincoln's eyes before he turned his head back and shut her out with his eyelids once again. Let him be angry. She was not going to offer him anything to eat, either. If he had changed his mind about the IV he could tell her about it. The doctor's notes said that he had been offered liquid food several times recently, and had become very angry when a nurse tried to force him to swallow some. She was going to see to it that he was positively drooling for something good-tasting before she offered him any chance at it.

'As you are doubtless aware,' Cassie said, when she had filled a washbasin for Lincoln's sponge bath, 'it will be very difficult for me to do anything but the front of you without your co-operation. However, I can manage to do it anyway. The only thing is, it may hurt more, even though I try to be careful. It's up to you. Now if you will turn a little bit . . .' She placed one hand under Lincoln's left shoulder. He lay there, inert as a cheese. 'OK, have it your way,' she said. She went to a cupboard where there was a supply of small, square pillows covered in waterproof film and picked up a stack. On the way back, she detected that Lincoln had opened his eyes a slit and was watching her.

'This is called the Lewis manoeuvre,' she said conversationally, 'invented when I had to work on one of the Chicago Bears, a middle linebacker I think he was, and the orderly who was supposed to help me didn't show up. I just keep tucking these under you until I get you where I want you. I can actually turn you clear over if I want to, but, of course, I don't want to do that yet. Maybe tomorrow.' She pulled a chair along and set the pile of pillows on it, then picked up Lincoln's left arm and laid it across his chest. Immediately he returned it to his side. Cassie picked it up again and held it firmly in her hands for a moment, running her fingers down his forearm in soothing strokes. 'Lincoln,' she said softly, 'leave your arm where I put it or I'll tape it to the hair on your chest.' This time the arm stayed.

Gradually, Cassie tucked pillows along Lincoln's back and buttocks until one side of his body was slightly elevated. After the second layer of pillows was in place, she noticed a small gap had appeared above them and that Lincoln's arm was much farther across his chest than it would have fallen by gravity alone. He was actually helping! At least he had the sense to see when he couldn't win by being stubborn. Cassie quickly wrung out the washcloth and went over Lincoln's large back and firm buttocks a little at a time, pausing frequently to dry an area and then apply a soothing lotion.

'Your skin's nice and smooth,' she commented, as she massaged the lotion on to the small of his back and below. 'You've still got a swimming-suit line.' She traced the line with her finger. 'I think it's a little lower than the one you had when I watched you boys going skinny-dipping down at the river.' She could feel

Lincoln's muscles tense beneath her hand and giggled. 'Didn't know I saw you, did you?' she said. 'I used to hang around up in the trees a lot when I was about seven or eight. You can see a lot of interesting things from up there. Maybe some day I'll tell you more. There are quite a lot. I know. I'll do like Scheherazade and tell you a new one each day. I'll let you guess how many days I can keep going without repeating myself.'

Cassie finished one side and removed the pillows. 'There. Now for the other side.' She grinned as Lincoln opened his eyes and quite frankly stared at her. 'Ah, Lincoln Snow,' she teased, 'how much I already know about you.' She did not really know a great deal first-hand, but from things she had overheard when she hung around, pestering her older brother, she knew that she could convincingly fabricate quite a few. And, if they were far enough from the truth, it might just provoke Lincoln into commenting.

It was noon by the time Cassie had finished bathing and shaving Lincoln, a tricky proposition going between the scars and stitches. 'There,' she said, when she had patted the last part of his chin dry. 'You look wonderful and I'm exhausted. Time for my lunch break.' She smoothed his hair back and sighed. 'I almost wish this were a double bed and I could call for room service. Almost, I said,' she added, when Lincoln again opened his eyes and stared at her. 'Take a little nap for me, too, will you? I'll be back in an hour. If you need me beforehand, just ring the bell. You know where the button is.'

Willton personally served Cassie her lunch, apologising for the canned soup and lack of proper table service. 'We are still trying to find some of the silver,' he said, frowning anxiously. 'I may have to call the senior Mrs Snow and ask where she may have stored it for safe keeping.'

'I don't want to discourage you, but, if she's like me, she put it somewhere she was sure to remember and then promptly forgot where that was,' Cassie said. 'I'm rather surprised they left it here at all.'

'No one expected Oak Hill to stay unused for so long,' Willton replied. 'I know that Mr Snow hoped to open it every summer, but his wife didn't like the country. It was a source of considerable friction between them.'

Poor Lincoln, Cassie thought. It sounded as if his personal life had not been a very happy one. 'How did Lincoln feel about New York City and his work there?' she asked.

'He enjoyed the cultural events,' Willton replied, 'but I don't think he regards his work as especially... well, perhaps I'm jumping to unwarranted conclusions, but my impression has been that his work was not of passionate interest to him, even though he has worked very hard and become a very influential market analyst. I have often thought that he needed to come back to Oak Hill in order to replenish his emotional resources. It's too bad that it took such a disastrous event to get him here.'

'And it was you who decided to come here?'

'Yes, it was,' Willton affirmed.

'I think it was a very wise move,' Cassie said. 'It may make all the difference.'

'Thank you,' Willton said, and for a moment his bright eyes misted over. 'I—I'd better see if Mrs

Comstock is back,' he said suddenly, and left the room.

There was no doubt how much Willton loved Lincoln Snow, Cassie thought, her heart going out to the loyal old man. How difficult it must have been for him to see so many things going awry for Lincoln and be unable to put them right.

Cassie sighed. There was no way to erase the past. But Lincoln had a lot of past before he went to New York, a past when she knew that he was happy. She could continue to recall that for him, and eventually try to get him to think about the future. How lovely it would be if he could stay at Oak Hill. His little daughter would doubtless thrive there, there were so many healthy things that a child could do in the out of doors. She needed to meet the little girl soon herself, and find out what she was like. But now she had better get back to her stubborn patient. The sooner she got him off his back and into the spring sunshine, the better off he would be, too.

When Cassie opened the bedroom door quietly and peeped in, she could see that Lincoln was actually asleep, rather than lying stiffly with his eyes closed. His head was turned against the pillow, his lips slightly parted, the hand that lay on top of the covers relaxed and open. Bless his heart, Cassie thought, feeling a rush of pleasure at the sight. Perhaps she had only exhausted him with her meticulous attentions, but it was the first time that anyone could report that he had even looked relaxed since the accident. 'Thrashes about and wakes himself up,' had been the most frequent comment. 'Can't seem to relax.' Of course, the pain was probably less intense now, too, Cassie reminded herself. It was hard to tell what the reason for his relaxed slumber might be. She tiptoed to the lounge chair in the corner of the room and sat down, leaning her own head back and closing her eyes. There wasn't anything that needed doing for at least another hour, and she had set the alarm on her watch to remind her of that.

It was the alarm that woke Cassie. She sat up straight with a start and looked over at her patient. Lincoln was awake, looking in her direction. He did not close his eyes, but watched as she got up and walked to his bedside.

'I got my nap after all,' she said, smiling at him. 'You were sleeping so soundly that I couldn't resist trying to catch forty winks. I got an hour, instead.' She bent over him and laid her hand against his forehead, stroking back his hair again very gently. 'You looked so nice and relaxed. I hope you feel that way still. I'm going to raise you up a bit now and then I'll do a little more work on your muscles. After the eternal thermometer and blood-pressure readings.'

This time, Lincoln did not look as if he was about to try and bite her if she put the thermometer in his mouth, so she inserted it under his tongue. He gave her no difficulty. She looked at her watch and then went to the window and looked out. The sun was shining, reflecting ripples from the brisk March wind on the pond.

'Things are beginning to get green,' she said. 'My dad's champing at the bit to get into the fields. As soon as it dries out enough he has some pasture to replant. But it's early yet. The robins aren't back. I expect they will be any day now. And that family of turkey vultures that lives by the river. They're such ugly big birds, but I do love to watch them soar. What must it be like to be able to fly like that? Have you ever noticed the way they use those feathers on their wing-tips just like fingers to turn the way they want to?' She checked her watch again and started back towards Lincoln, surprised to see that he was still following her with his eyes very closely. She looked from him to the window and back. 'I'm going to get your bed moved so that you can see outside,' she said. 'It's ridiculous, in this place, to have nothing to look at but the ceiling. Of course,' she added, as she retrieved the thermometer, 'you're going to be getting around in a wheelchair before very long. Then we can go outside and get some sunshine and fresh air. Real air. Not that thick stuff they have in Chicago and New York.'

For the next two hours, Cassie worked continuously, manipulating Lincoln's muscles where there were no bruises or breaks to prevent it.

She brought out some of her little pillows again, expecting Lincoln to lie there in uncooperative silence. To her surprise, once she had a few pillows in place he actually made an effort to turn himself on his side in spite of his still painful ribs.

'Terrific,' Cassie complimented him, slathering the massaging lotion on to her hands and then beginning to rub down his back. 'Of course, if you're like me you'd walk across hot coals for a good back-rub. My idea of a dream husband would be one who would give me a perfect back-rub at least once a day.'

When she had finished, she picked up a fresh pile of pillows. 'I'm going to tuck these under your left side,' she said as she did so, 'and then let you have some relief from my company while I go to dinner. It's best if you don't lie flat all the time, as I'm sure you are aware. There.' She tucked Lincoln's covers over him and stood up, running her hands across her moist forehead beneath her reddish-blonde bangs. He looked so small and vulnerable lying there, with just his head and the arm with the IV showing, even though she knew he was over six feet tall. Her arms ached to hold him close and comfort him as he had held her that day so long ago.

'Try and take another nap,' she said, her voice husky with emotion. 'I'll be back very soon.'

Long before Cassie reached the morning-room, where she was to have dinner, her nose told her that Mrs Comstock had definitely found the wherewithal to make dinner. If Lincoln could smell that, he'd probably begin to feel differently about eating, she thought to herself. Too bad she couldn't take a huge bag full of that odour back upstairs with her.

'I see Mrs Comstock got her potatoes,' Cassie remarked to Willton, as he served her roast beef and mashed potatoes with dark brown gravy. 'This looks wonderful.'

'I do believe she will work out as a cook,' Willton agreed. 'Not cordon bleu, but certainly very good. The type of food Mr Snow will like, if he will only...' Willton stopped, looking pained and unhappy.

'I'm going to start working on that,' Cassie said quickly. 'I have a plan. If the doctor will go along with it, I'll tell you later.' Willton hovered near the table, as if he wanted to stay but was reluctant to place himself in the position of a dinner companion for Cassie. 'Sit down, Willton, and keep me company,' she said, sensing that he might have something to tell her. 'Have you thought of something that I should know?'

Willton pulled out a chair and sat down, still looking somewhat anxious. 'I don't know quite how to say this,' he said, 'but perhaps it is relevant. Mr Tyler and Mr Snow had not been getting along at all well before the accident. It seemed that Mr Tyler could never manage to stay within his allowance, which was quite a princely sum, I believe. The young man is twenty years old now, and has never managed to finish school or find employment. I'm afraid Mr Snow was far too lenient with him after Mrs Snow's death. Of course, he had a great deal on his mind then, with the child and all.'

'Tyler always knew how to make himself completely obnoxious,' Cassie commented. 'I guess he hasn't changed.' Cassie thought about what Willton had said for a few minutes, trying to read between the lines. Suddenly a fearful thought sent a chill through her. Could Tyler have become really ugly, rather than just unbearable? 'Were they having a disagreement before the accident?' she asked. 'Are you implying that it might not have been an accident?'

'I wasn't there, Miss Cassandra,' Willton replied stiffly. 'All I know is that, as soon as he was able, Mr Snow told the authorities it was an accident. He tripped and tumbled through a weak section of the railing around the penthouse veranda. However, I have never known Mr Snow to be clumsy, and he certainly did not drink to excess that night or any other night. But nor can I imagine him lying to protect the young man if he was...seriously involved. I must confess, I don't know quite what to believe.'

I'm afraid I do, Cassie thought grimly. Tyler might not have meant it to happen, but she thought him quite capable of taking a swing at Lincoln if Lincoln thwarted his desires. And then again, Tyler might have actually... No, she'd better not jump to that conclusion just because she loathed Tyler. She looked at Willton. 'Whatever is bothering Lincoln is very serious,' she said. 'I think we both know he wouldn't be so upset over a simple accident.'

Willton knotted his hands together in front of him and looked down. 'Yes, Miss Cassandra,' he agreed, 'we do know that. However,' he looked up at her again, 'we mustn't rule out the possibility that something I know nothing about may have been the cause. I'm not privy to every detail of Mr Snow's life.'

Cassie gave him a sideways look. 'I doubt that you miss very much, Willton,' she said, amused at the slightly guilty look on the old man's face.

Willton excused himself while Cassie finished her dinner, at the same time trying to figure out how Lincoln's strange reluctance to try to get better might be related to something Tyler had done. If Tyler had actually had something to do with Lincoln's fall, how would Lincoln react? If it were her, she would climb out of bed with her casts on and bludgeon Tyler with her crutch, but the Lincoln she knew was not like that. He would more likely be heartbroken and disappointed that he had so completely failed to turn Tyler into a decent human being. That hypothesis seemed to fit quite well with the sadness that Cassie felt was underlying Lincoln's stubborn reluctance to eat or talk. If worse came to worst, she would ask him about Tyler.

She had just reached that conclusion when Willton returned with freshly baked chocolate cake and coffee. 'Good heavens, cake too?' she exclaimed. 'I'm already stuffed. I think I'll take it upstairs with me, if you don't mind, and have it later. In fact, I think I'll take my coffee with me now, too.' It was marvellously fragrant coffee, and Cassie thought that bringing it into Lincoln's room might stimulate some desire for something other than his IV fluid. 'Does Lincoln usually like coffee?' she asked.

'Oh, my goodness, yes,' Willton replied. 'He's a regular connoisseur of fine coffee. Perhaps if he smells that ...'

'Just what I was thinking,' Cassie said. She picked up her coffee and cake. 'Dr Norton should be here soon. Would you bring me another cup of coffee then, please? I always like a second cup.'

'Certainly, Miss Cassandra,' Willton replied, a twinkle in his eyes. 'I do believe you're going to have Mr Snow on the mend in spite of himself.'

'I hope so, Willton,' Cassie said. 'But I'd rather it was because he wanted to be well.'

CHAPTER THREE

LINCOLN was awake when Cassie returned, looking, she thought, a bit uncomfortable. She set her coffee and cake on his bedside table and quickly removed the pillows behind him, and then raised his bed. 'There, is that better?' she asked. 'I could tell you were getting uncomfortable.' She picked up her coffee and took a sip. 'Mrs Comstock makes great coffee,' she said. 'Take a whiff.' She held the cup under Lincoln's nose for a moment. 'Willton thinks she'll work out all right as a cook. Her roast beef and gravy was excellent, too. I haven't tried her chocolate cake yet, though.' She picked it up and showed it to Lincoln. 'I was too stuffed to appreciate it, so I thought I'd save it until a little later. Now, we'd better do the thermometer and blood-pressure routine one more time before Dr Norton gets here.'

Cassie quickly turned her back on Lincoln and went to get a new thermometer, afraid that she might burst out laughing. His expression when she had held the coffee under his nose and then shown him the cake had been almost funny. His eyes had grown bigger, and he had been unable to keep from moistening his lips with his tongue. If that was any indication, her idea wouldn't take long to work.

When the doctor arrived to look over Lincoln and his records for the day, Cassie took her new cup of coffee and stood nearby, sipping it thoughtfully. She saw Lincoln staring at her, his eyes now narrowed, as if he understood what she was up to and was trying to tell her it wouldn't work. She grinned at him unrepentantly. 'My, but this is good coffee,' she said.

The doctor looked up, then back and forth between Cassie and Lincoln. He raised his eyebrows, but said nothing. When he had finished, he asked Cassie to accompany him down the hall so that he could talk to her. 'Certainly, Doctor,' Cassie replied. 'I have something to ask you about.'

'Mr Snow is looking quite a bit better this evening,' Dr Norton said as soon as they were alone. 'I'm not sure what you've done, but keep it up. I'm especially pleased that his blood-pressure is normal and his colour is better. Has he spoken to you at all?'

'Not yet,' Cassie replied with a sigh. 'However, I have an idea I'd like you to approve that might kill two birds with one stone, so to speak.'

'Oh? What is that?' the doctor asked.

'I'd like to remove his IV later tonight. By morning, he should be quite hungry and thirsty, but I'm going to tell him when the IV comes out that he'll have to ask me for something to eat or drink. I'm not going to try to force anything on him. I'm just going to have my own food served in his room, and make sure it's something that smells delectable.'

For a moment, Dr Norton frowned at Cassie. Then he burst out laughing. 'That's almost diabolical,' he said. 'I saw his face when you were drinking your coffee. All right, but don't let him go without fluids for too long.'

'No, sir,' Cassie said. 'I'll be very careful about that.'

Cassie returned to Lincoln's bedside. He was lying with his eyes closed tightly and his hand clenched, looking anything but relaxed. 'Something bothering you?' Cassie asked, picking up her cake and starting to eat it. 'Mmm. Good cake.'

Lincoln opened his eyes and glared at her. For a moment, Cassie thought he was going to speak, but then he closed his eyes again.

'Grouch,' Cassie said. 'I spend my entire day with someone who's about as entertaining as a box of rocks and you have the nerve to glare at me just because I'm enjoying a piece of chocolate cake. Darned ungrateful, if you ask me. If you have any imagination at all, try putting my shoes on. I'd be glad to try yours, if you'd talk to me.' She finished her cake and coffee and set the dishes aside. 'I hope you don't mind if we watch the late news,' she said, picking up the remote control for the television set across the room. 'I'd like to know if the rest of the world is still out there. After that, I'll have some news for you.'

While the news programme was on, Cassie sat in the straight chair next to Lincoln's bed. He opened his eyes once or twice, but gave no indication of interest in the events of the day, in spite of the fact that one of the major stories concerned the stock market, the field in which he had worked for some years. When the programme was over, Cassie stood up, took a deep breath and mentally crossed her fingers. She hoped she wasn't going too fast, trying to get Lincoln to start moving out of his recalcitrant, stony silence and begin to eat at the same time, but it seemed to her that the longer she waited, the more difficult it would become, for he might get the idea that she was willing to put up with his behaviour indefinitely.

She leaned over Lincoln's bed, and brushed his hair back from his forehead. 'Lincoln,' she said, 'would you please look at me? I have something important to tell you.' When he did not comply, she reached around and pinched his ear. That brought an immediate response of a frown, but also partly opened eyes. 'That's better,' Cassie said. 'The news I mentioned earlier is this. I am now, with Dr Norton's approval, going to take out your IV. By morning, if not sooner, you will become quite hungry and thirsty. Now, you may think that I am trying to force you to eat and drink on your own, but that's not true at all. I wouldn't think of such a thing. I am simply trying to provide you with an opportunity to enjoy Mrs Comstock's excellent cooking. However, I won't give you anything at all unless you ask for it. You can lie here panting like a sheepdog for all I care, wasting away to a nubbin. Of course, I had to promise the doctor I wouldn't let things go too far, but believe me, you'll feel a lot better if you don't see how far I will go.'

Cassie smiled as Lincoln's stoic expression changed to a glare. 'Good,' she said. 'Two glares in one evening. That beats the absolute blank. Now, you may be asking yourself, Why didn't she just go along with things for a bit longer? That coffee smelled so good tonight. I might have decided in a week or two that I was going to try some. The answer, dear Lincoln, is that I lied to you when I said I had the patience of a saint. I have very little. And, there is no reason for you to go on like this. You have a problem to solve. I don't know what it is, but we'll certainly not make any headway unless you talk to me or whoever else you want to talk to about it. Have you anything to say on your behalf before I disconnect you from that infernal device?' When Lincoln did not, she shrugged.

'All right, then. I'm not going to leave anything in your arm, either. No point in making it too easy to go backwards.'

With that, Cassie shut off the fluid, and then very carefully removed the needle from Lincoln's arm. 'There we are,' she said. 'You won't be getting any pain-killer, either, so you may want that before morning. I have some that will be easy for you to swallow, so just ring if you want it. Don't try to be macho and tough it out. You need your rest.'

She lowered Lincoln's bed, then bent over him again. There was a suspicious moistness at the corners of his closed eyes, and Cassie felt an immediate agonising pain in her own heart.

'Oh, Lincoln,' she murmured softly, taking her fingertips and wiping away the tears, 'please don't think I'm cruel and unfeeling. I care so much about you. I have for a long time. Ever since that time you cared enough to bring me that puppy. Remember?'

At that, Lincoln opened his eyes and looked at Cassie. For a moment, looking into his misty eyes, she felt as if she were back on that roadside long ago, discovering for the first time that a man could feel such deep sorrow at another's loss. He stared at her for a long time, a look so intent and searching that she felt as if he were trying very hard to discover something in her face that might tell him whether she really meant what she said. At last he nodded, ever so slightly. 'I remember,' he said.

The surge of happiness that filled Cassie's heart at those simple words set her to blinking away triumphant tears of happiness from her own eyes. 'He's still around, old Monty II,' she said. 'I'll take you to see him some time soon. Now try to sleep, but, if you need me, remember that I'm in the adjoining room, and the door will be open. You can ring or yell at me, I don't care which. I'll be right here.'

Cassie turned out the lights, then went into her own room. Before she got ready for bed she stood by the window, looking out on the peaceful scene of the countryside at night, a partial moon rising behind the house sending soft, long shadows across the pond. She had made a lot of headway with Lincoln already, but there was still a long way to go. What could have happened to make him so reluctant to go on with his life? Something, or, more likely, someone, had hurt him deeply. How could they? Even that disgusting Tyler must know that Lincoln was the kindest of men. She sighed. Perhaps that was the problem. Being kind was not always the best answer. She had had to make Lincoln think she was unkind before she got any response at all from him. It still remained to be seen if he would co-operate in any other ways, and if he didn't . . .

'I'll cross that bridge when I get there,' Cassie murmured. Right now, she had better get some sleep. This could be a very trying night, for she had every intention of checking frequently to make sure that Lincoln was all right.

Cassie had checked twice, each time finding that Lincoln was apparently asleep. She felt, when the noisy buzzer sounded, as if she had only just dropped off to sleep again, but a bleary look towards her windows revealed the vague greyness of dawn.

'I'm coming,' she called, grabbing her robe and pushing her feet into her slippers in one movement. When she got to the doorway, she could see Lincoln clearly, raised up on one elbow. No matter what the

cause, she was a little relieved to see that he had moved
more on his own than he had since the accident. 'What
can I do for you?' she asked, turning on the light next
to his bed.

'Thirsty,' he replied.

Cassie quickly filled a water glass and put in a straw,
holding it close for Lincoln to drink. She could see
the lines of strain deeply chiselled around his eyes.
He was in pain, no doubt the effort of raising himself
after so long not helping any. He finished the drink
and lay back, closing his eyes and sighing deeply.

'I can tell that you're in pain,' she said. 'Can I give
you something for it?'

He opened his eyes again. 'What?' he asked.

'Nothing you couldn't give a child, unless you want
something stronger,' she replied. 'This is it. She held
up a bottle of liquid pain medicine. 'It's not even pre-
scription. Do you want some?' When Lincoln nodded,
she got a spoon and opened the bottle. 'I'll give you
a little more than I would a child,' she said, smiling
at him. 'It goes by weight.' When he had swallowed
the medicine she went on, 'That should help within
fifteen minutes. Do you want another drink to wash
it down?' Lincoln shook his head. 'All right,' Cassie
said, 'but I'll refill your water glass and leave it on
the table. You can reach it yourself, if you feel so
inclined.'

Back in her bed, Cassie stretched and yawned. She
felt as if she had hardly been to sleep at all, and it
would be time to get up before very long. Still, she
was so happy at Lincoln's progress that she didn't
mind. If only she could keep him moving forward.
Surely he was beginning to see that it would accom-
plish nothing to keep resisting the process of healing

that his body was carrying on in spite of him? If only he would begin to take some real nourishment in the morning...

Lincoln was sleeping soundly when Cassie went into his room, ready to begin the day's routine. He had not touched the glass of water, but she was not surprised. With only one good arm it would have put quite a strain on his ribs to sit up and reach for it. No doubt he would be very thirsty when he awoke. Instead of awakening him, she scurried down the stairs to tell Mrs Comstock to prepare an especially flavourful clear soup for Lincoln, in hopes that he would soon ask for it, and she left instructions for her own breakfast to be brought to Lincoln's room as soon as it was ready. When she returned to his room, he was again propped on one elbow, staring balefully in the direction of her door. The glass of water lay shattered on the floor.

'I should have known you'd wake up the minute I left,' Cassie said, hurrying to find another glass for him. 'Are you thirsty?'

'Yes,' Lincoln replied. He drank the water quickly.

'More pain medicine?' Cassie asked.

'No,' Lincoln replied.

'Hungry?' Cassie asked.

Lincoln shut his eyes and said nothing. Cassie's heart sank. Obviously, he was still determined to be stubborn about eating. Well, she would soon see if the smell of fresh coffee and bacon would change that. She ordinarily ate cereal for breakfast, but that would have little aroma to stimulate Lincoln's taste buds, so she had asked for bacon and eggs and toast.

Willton, himself, brought Cassie's breakfast tray.

'Good morning, Miss Cassandra,' he said formally. 'Good morning, sir.' He looked at Lincoln, who made no response.

Cassie shrugged and gave Willton a despairing look. The old man nodded, and quickly retreated. When he had gone, Cassie tried for a moment to control her impatience, then blurted, 'Lincoln Snow, there is no excuse for your treating Willton that way! That dear old man would give his life for you. What possible excuse can you have for acting as if he weren't even here?'

When Lincoln still made no response, Cassie ground her teeth together to control her seething temper. You must try to be patient, she told herself over and over. You're just frustrated. Don't push too hard. You don't know what's going on in Lincoln's mind. Maybe he thinks he does have a reason. Maybe he really does. Nothing she could say to herself made her feel any less angry. She drank her coffee, but had no appetite for the food. She banged the cup down noisily on the tray.

'I'd hoped to have a pleasant companion for breakfast, but now you've gone and ruined my appetite,' she growled, glaring in Lincoln's direction. 'I hope you're satisfied. Maybe we can starve together. That should make interesting headlines. Nurse and Wall Street tycoon in apparent suicide pact. No reason for their refusal to eat given, and neither will comment. Perhaps sympathy with the starving children of Ethiopia has led this misguided couple——'

'Shut up, Cassie,' Lincoln said, opening his eyes and glaring at her.

'Well, well. He talks,' Cassie snapped. She bent over Lincoln and stared, close range, into his eyes. 'I will not shut up, Lincoln dear. The only way you will shut me up is to talk so much that I can't get a word in edgeways. So there!'

Lincoln's glare faded a little towards thought-fulness as he stared back at Cassie. 'No one could talk that much,' he said finally, before he closed his eyes again.

Cassie was at first startled, then she burst out laughing. 'At least your wits haven't completely left you,' she said. 'But you're wrong. My last patient, a sweet little old lady named Millicent Sedgewick, did it all the time.'

The rest of the morning went quite smoothly. While Cassie had her mid-morning coffee in his room, a muscular young black man named Max, a horti-culture student whom Willton had hired to bring order back to the beautiful grounds and gardens at Oak Hill, came and moved Lincoln's bed so that he could, if he liked, see out of the window. Although he did not immediately take advantage of the opportunity, Cassie thought that he might do so when he thought she wasn't looking, in order to preserve his stubbornly recalcitrant image. He continued to drink water quite often. But when Cassie's lunch was brought, and along with it a large cup of wonderful-smelling soup for Lincoln, he still showed no inclination to have any. Cassie managed to refrain from making any comment, but she wondered to herself how much longer he could hold out, and how much longer she should continue to deny him any nourishment. She was very much afraid that if he had taken none by that night, Dr

Norton would tell her to restart the intravenous feeding.

By late afternoon, Lincoln's stomach was growling frequently and Cassie's nerves were so taut that she ached from the strain of keeping silent about it. When her dinner and Lincoln's soup were brought she could keep quiet no longer.

'I really think that you should try a little of this,' she said, holding the soup where he could inhale its aroma. When Lincoln only stubbornly pursed his mouth and closed his eyes, she felt something inside of her give way. This, she decided, was it. Something had to give and, if it was not going to be without a struggle, so be it. She set the soup down on her tray, marched over to the door, and locked it.

'There,' she said, turning back to face Lincoln, who was now watching her. 'I've locked the door, so that no one can disturb us. We're going to have this out, right now, just you and me. First of all, let's get rid of that fiction about your having had an accident. You wouldn't be lying there, refusing to eat, just because you're so shattered at finding out that you have two left feet. It has something to do with that miserable Tyler Spenser, doesn't it?'

'It was an accident!' Lincoln denied, quite loudly.

'Oh, sure,' Cassie retorted even louder. 'I'll believe that when I see a herd of elephants come charging across that field out there!' She waved her hand towards the meadow beyond the pond. 'I should have held that miserable little monster under water that time that I pushed him into the pond!'

'Cassie!' Lincoln said warningly. 'I don't know what Willton's been telling you, but——'

'He hasn't told me anything I didn't already know,'
Cassie interrupted. 'All he said was that he doesn't
know what happened, that you and Tyler had been
arguing before that, and that no one's seen hide nor
hair of him since your accident.' She took a deep
breath, her eyes locked on to those of Lincoln, who
was looking at her as if he were seeing some kind of
strange apparition. 'Why are you looking at me like
that? Just because I'm blundering in where angels
feared to tread? Someone has to. I can't let you lie
here, destroying yourself, for no reason. Starving
yourself isn't going to help anyone, least of all Tyler.
Are you hoping he'll feel remorse and come to your
bedside? Fat chance!'

'Cassie!' Lincoln said again. 'Just be quiet. You
don't know what you're talking about?'

'Oh? Do you mean all of this strange behaviour of
yours has nothing to do with Tyler? If that's the case,
speak up. I'll listen.' When Lincoln made no reply,
Cassie smiled grimly. 'All right, then you listen to me,
Lincoln Snow. I know Tyler a lot better than you
think. Do you know why I pitched him into the pond
that day? It wasn't just for a lark, believe me. I
seriously hoped that he would sink to the bottom and
never come up, and I didn't feel that way just because
he teased and did nasty little tricks all the time, either.
Let me tell you what that little monster did. Two days
before that party, which was an Easter egg hunt, Tyler
came over to see the baby rabbits I was raising because he knew that I was going to bring some to the
party for the children to see. Like a fool, I let him
hold one, after warning him to be very careful about
squeezing them too tightly. And that, Lincoln Snow,
is exactly what he did. He took that darling little

animal and squeezed the life right out of it, right in front of my eyes, then dropped it on the ground and grinned at me! Then, when I got hysterical and upset, he had the nerve to tell my mother that—and I quote— it was so adorable that he just loved it too much!'

By now, Cassie's eyes were filled with tears at the memory of that pitiful event. 'My mother,' she went on, angrily dashing the tears from her cheeks, 'tried to tell me that he didn't know what he was doing, that he certainly wouldn't have done it on purpose, but if she'd been there and seen his face she would have known what really happened. I'll never forget that look as long as I live, and I've seen some pretty awful things, working in a big city hospital emergency-room, believe me. So save your pity, or anguish, or whatever it is you're feeling, for someone who's worth it. I don't care what happened that night, I don't want to know what happened unless you want to tell me, but for heaven's sake, don't keep torturing yourself. Eat some of your soup. Please.'

Cassie pulled out a Kleenex and wiped her eyes while she watched Lincoln, who had turned his head to look out of the window, his expression sad, but not withdrawn now. It was, she thought, almost as if he were seeing something outside, perhaps the memory of that Easter party in that very spot. If only he would say something, she thought desperately, silently pleading with him to try and understand what she had tried to tell him. Perhaps she had been wrong to bring up that terrible thing that Tyler had done. Maybe she had only made things worse...

'All right, Cassie,' Lincoln said, turning his head and looking up at her. 'I'll eat some soup.'

'You will?' Cassie blinked back tears of relief and gave him a wavering smile. 'You really will? I mean, you don't mean just this once? You'll start to eat now, and get back on regular food soon? Promise?'

Lincoln nodded. 'I will. I promise.'

Cassie's tears started to flow in earnest. 'I'm sorry. I'm ... just so glad,' she gulped, mopping her tears again and then reaching for the soup, which was in a tall mug with a heavy glass drinking tube in it. 'Now, don't drink this too fast,' she said, her hand shaking as she started to hold it out towards Lincoln's mouth.

'Wait a minute. Put that down,' Lincoln said. 'Just for a minute,' he added, as Cassie's face fell. 'Sit down here.' He patted the side of his bed and held out his hand towards Cassie.

Cassie sat down and took his hand. 'You're going to bawl me out, aren't you?' she said apprehensively.

'No, I certainly am not,' Lincoln said. He took Cassie's hand and held it against his cheek. 'You're a strange woman, Cassie,' he said, his eyes warm and bright with more light than Cassie had ever seen in them, a light so soft and loving that she felt as dizzy as she had the day she had written in her diary that Lincoln Snow had smiled at her.

'You're not exactly Mr Average American yourself,' she said, looking down in confusion for fear that he would see too much of the warmth and joy that suddenly set her heart racing, as if the love she had thought gone had lain there, waiting to be rekindled, since she was only fourteen.

'I know,' Lincoln agreed. 'You and I,' he went on slowly, 'may not quite agree on what Tyler is worth, but there's no doubt that we agree on the fact that his behaviour is atrocious.' He slid his hand up

Cassie's arm and put his hand behind her shoulder. 'Put your head on my shoulder,' he said. 'You need someone to hold you right now.' When Cassie hesitated, staring at him, he added, 'Go ahead, it won't hurt my ribs.' He put a slight pressure on Cassie's back and she leaned over and did as he asked, sighing deeply. 'How, on God's earth, anyone could hurt either you or a little animal like that, I can't imagine. Especially you.' Lincoln leaned his cheek against Cassie's hair and patted her back. 'Especially you,' he repeated softly.

Cassie held very still in the curve of Lincoln's comforting arm, trying to keep her weight from pressing too hard against him. At the same time, she felt such a strong surge of emotion that it was difficult for her to do anything but lie against him and revel in the feelings of warmth and happiness that filled her. At last she pushed herself away, saying hoarsely, 'Thank you. But I'm not a child any more. I'm supposed to be taking care of you.'

Lincoln kept his hand behind Cassie's neck, preventing her from sitting upright, his fingers toying with her hair. 'I'm well aware that you're not a child,' he said, his eyes caressing Cassie's face and resting lingeringly on her lips. 'You're as beautiful a woman as I always knew you'd be.'

He wants to kiss me, Cassie thought, as their eyes held each other motionless. Her heart was pounding. She wanted to kiss him so much! It was hardly the right thing for her to do, but . . . She leaned forward experimentally, and Lincoln's hand came along, encouraging her. Oh, lord, I can't help myself, Cassie thought desperately, just before she closed her eyes and pressed her lips to Lincoln's.

The touch of Lincoln's lips was the sweetest Cassie had ever felt, as gentle and loving as the man himself. It made her feel as if spring had suddenly come into full bloom inside her heart, conjuring up promises of even more beautiful days to come. Reluctantly, she pulled back and smiled tremulously at Lincoln.

'I—I really shouldn't have done that,' she said, 'but I can't truthfully say I'm sorry.'

Lincoln smiled, the first time he had really smiled since Cassie had come to be with him. 'Neither am I. Thank you, Cassie. That's the nicest thing that's happened to me in a long, long time.'

CHAPTER FOUR

For the next two weeks, Lincoln made steady progress. He was soon back to eating regular 'people' food, as he called it. All but one line of stitches was removed from his face. His hair grew rapidly, almost covering the evidence of his nearly healed wound. He began spending progressively longer times sitting in a chair each day, with the muscular Max helping him in and out of his bed. When he actually grumbled that he was going to be 'damned glad to get these casts off', Cassie was elated.

'Your arm will be out soon,' she told him. 'As soon as it gets some strength back, you can try your crutches. In the meantime, I have a surprise for you. Max is going to put you in your wheelchair today, and then we'll go outside for a little while. That lift your grandfather had put in when he got arthritis is going to come in very handy. I'm not sure even Max could carry you up the stairs alone. You're beginning to put some weight back on.'

For a moment, Lincoln looked as though he was about to reject the idea, looking outside and frowning.

'It's a beautiful day. The temperature is in the sixties, and the robins are back,' Cassie said hopefully. 'There were some ducks on the pond when I got up this morning.'

'All right,' Lincoln said at last, giving her a wistful smile. 'It's just not my idea of fun to be pushed around in a wheelchair.'

'It won't be necessary for long,' Cassie replied quickly. 'You'll be back on your own two feet again before you know it.'

There had been no more discussion of Tyler Spenser, and Cassie had deemed it best to let the topic alone. She could tell that something was still disturbing Lincoln deeply, for he would sometimes lapse into a brooding silence, making only minimal replies to her questions, and scarcely seeming to hear what she said if she told him something she thought might interest him.

One afternoon an old schoolfriend of Lincoln's stopped by to visit him, and Cassie took advantage of the opportunity to finally go to the nursery, a huge room in the other wing of the house, and meet Colleen, whom she had seen several times from a distance when her nanny had her outside.

'She's a handful,' Mrs Lindstrom, her nanny, confessed, while the red-haired tyke swung off on her crutches to fetch her favourite doll to show Cassie. 'That red hair really means a temper. She's always been able to wrap her daddy around her little finger.'

'Are you my daddy's nurse?' Colleen asked, when Cassie had finished admiring her Raggedy Ann doll. Her speech was somewhat slurred, but not as difficult to understand as Cassie had expected it might be from what Willton had told her of the child's handicap.

'Yes, I am,' Cassie replied. 'Your daddy's getting a lot better. He should be able to come and see you very soon.' Cassie had suggested once to Lincoln that he might like to have Colleen visit him, but he had rejected that idea very firmly. He did not want her to think that he was an invalid, he said. It was going to be hard enough for her to cope with his scarred face, which couldn't be repaired for some time yet.

'You tell him I want him to come and see me today,' Colleen said, jerking her little chin up as if she expected Cassie to agree with her demands immediately. 'I'm tired of waiting for him to get better.'

'I'll tell him you said that,' Cassie agreed, 'but I don't think he's quite ready to come and see you. The doctor hasn't told him that he can yet.'

Colleen scowled, apparently mulling over what Cassie had said. 'Does he have to do what the doctor says?' she asked.

'Yes, he does,' Cassie replied. 'Just as you and I do.'

'I don't always,' Colleen said, giving Cassie a sideways look. 'Sometimes I don't eat my breakfast cereal.'

Cassie repressed a smile. There was obviously a defiant spirit inside that tiny body. 'That's pretty serious,' she said. 'You've got to eat plenty to grow on.'

'I'm never going to grow very much, anyway,' Colleen said, her face turning sullen. 'I heard the doctor say so. And I won't be pretty like you are, so it doesn't matter if I eat my breakfast or not.'

Poor little thing, Cassie thought. What a lot of unpleasant realities she had already had to face. But, with those red-gold curls and that happy smile, she would win the hearts of any but the most unfeeling. 'I think that the doctor just meant that you're going to be a small person,' Cassie said, 'not that you weren't going to grow just like anyone else. And as for being pretty, I hope you don't think that a brace on your leg makes any difference.'

Colleen made a face. 'My mouth's funny, too, and one of my arms isn't right. I'm not ever gonna be pretty.'

Cassie beckoned to Colleen, who frowned curiously and came to stand in front of her. Cassie looked her over very seriously from head to foot, then took Colleen's chin in her hand and peered into her lovely green eyes.

After a moment, Colleen jerked her head away and scowled. 'Whatcha doin' that for?' she asked.

'Because,' Cassie replied, 'my mother always told me that pretty was inside you, and the only place to look for it was in a person's eyes. She said that pretty was being good and kind and loving, and ugly was being mean and cross and bad. You can usually tell by a person's eyes which they are. Not always, though. Sometimes a person can fool you.'

Colleen's eyes grew wide. 'Can you tell about me?' she asked.

'I think so,' Cassie answered seriously. 'I think there's a lot of pretty in you, but there might be a little cross in there too. Maybe you'd better work on that.' She stood up, ruffling the hair of the little girl, who was staring at her, open-mouthed. 'Now, I'd better get back to your daddy. Maybe some day soon you'd like to come and visit my daddy's farm and see the baby animals. We can have my mother look you over and see if she thinks you're pretty or not. She's the real expert. Would you like that?'

'Yeah.' Colleen nodded vigorously and smiled her slightly crooked smile. 'I'll make sure there isn't any cross in my eyes at all.'

'Good.' Cassie ruffled Colleen's curls again and then went to see how Lincoln and his friend were getting along. Lincoln had seemed pleased to see the man, but she knew that his tolerance for idle conversation was not very great. She was going to have to get him primed to survive Pat Wanamaker, the substitute nurse who was going to be here tomorrow while Cassie went to see Ogden Warren. Pat, the mother of an old schoolmate of Cassie's, would doubtless gossip non-stop about the inhabitants of White Oak county.

'She can't possibly be any worse than you are, as excited as you seem to be over seeing old Oggie Warren,' Lincoln commented good-naturedly from behind his newspaper the next morning when Cassie warned him about Pat Wanamaker. 'My ears are numb already.'

'Hmm. Numb ears. I'll have to report that to Dr Norton,' Cassie teased. 'Lend me an arm. I need to take your blood-pressure.'

Lincoln sighed and put down his newspaper. 'When will this blood-pressure taking ever end? I can't even read my paper in peace.'

'Soon enough,' Cassie replied, putting on the cuff and pumping it up. 'Are you that eager to get rid of me?' She had been thinking about that eventuality herself, as Lincoln's condition improved rapidly, and found that she did not like the prospect at all. Neither, apparently, did Lincoln.

'Hell, no!' he barked. 'I don't want to get rid of you at all.'

'Ouch!' Cassie cried, pulling her stethoscope from her ears. 'Good lord, I think you just deafened me.'

'I'm sorry,' Lincoln said quickly. 'Just don't startle me like that with such unpleasant thoughts. I haven't decided how to deal with that one yet, but one thing's for certain: I'm not going to let you go.'

'Y-you're not?' Cassie stammered, staring at him. His eyes held that lovely, glowing light that always made her feel as if the ground were swaying beneath her feet.

Lincoln shook his head. 'As soon as I'm really all back together, we'll have to do some very serious talking about that. Meanwhile, don't even think about leaving.'

'All right,' Cassie said, her words coming out in a hoarse whisper. What on earth did Lincoln mean, that he wasn't going to let her go? He wasn't going to need a nurse for much longer, and she had no other skills for which he might employ her. He was definitely not the type to want her to stay around as a live-in lover, especially not with his little girl in the house, and he must know that she would not like that idea either. Not with her own parents less than a mile away. He couldn't mean that he was thinking of marriage. Could he? A little dazed by that idea, Cassie had to pump the blood-pressure sleeve up twice to get her reading. Apparently, whatever Lincoln had in mind, it had his physiology in high gear, too, for his blood-pressure was higher than normal.

'Have you been jogging when I wasn't looking?' she asked, frowning at him with mock suspicion.

Lincoln smiled. 'No, but I've been covering a lot of ground mentally,' he replied. 'Why? Is my blood-pressure up?'

'Just a little,' Cassie answered. 'I expect listening to Pat Wanamaker will lull you back to a dormant state.'

*　　*　　*

It took Cassie some time to shift gears and begin thinking about the stage, an environment so different from the one she had been in with Lincoln. The look in Lincoln's eyes when he had said that he would not let her go haunted her as she drove into Midvale and parked near the auditorium wing where the theatre department had their offices. It was so strange, the way she felt when he looked at her like that. The luminous brightness of his eyes made her feel as if he had penetrated deep inside her, almost merging his heart and mind with hers, like some alien from another planet with powers far exceeding those of mortal men.

Then Cassie knocked on Ogden Warren's door and was jolted by another strange sensation when he opened it and cried out enthusiastically, 'Cassie, my dear, do come in.' Seeing a man she had known as a chubby-faced beardless boy now sporting a devilish black pointed beard and speaking with a British accent took all of her resources to keep a straight face.

'Ogden, you look marvellous,' she said, taking the initiative to keep herself on track. 'Almost another Vincent Price.'

'Oh, but my dear,' Ogden said, beaming and taking both of her hands in his, '*you* are the transformation. What a beauty you've become! To think that I once tried to put a snake down your back! And I've heard nothing but good reports of your thespian talents. I think this is going to be a most happy reunion.'

Ogden led Cassie to a seat by the desk in his cluttered office and once again went through the things he had talked to Cassie about on the telephone, this time bringing out sketches and pages of figures to detail the planning he had gone through in order to get the Shakespeare Festival off the ground. *Macbeth* and *As You Like It* were the productions planned in addition to *The Taming of the Shrew*. 'To keep it light and familiar this first year,' Ogden explained.

'I'm extremely impressed, Ogden,' Cassie said when he finally paused for breath. 'You've done a wonderful job.'

'Thank you, love,' Ogden said, looking very pleased. 'I'm not going to pretend with you, Cassie,' he went on. 'I've done most of the work so far, but I can't keep it up, not once we're in production. My great love is directing. What I'd like to find, if God would be so good to me, is a couple of really good actors who can double in production and planning. There would be year-round work here for them. Not fancy salaries, of course, but if we're a success it would be very rewarding. If you think you could qualify and might be interested in such a job, you'd be in on the ground floor. I'm not above putting an old friend in the front of the pack.'

If she might be interested! Cassie restrained an impulse to hug Ogden Warren, instead saying carefully, 'There's nothing I'd like better, Ogden. I'm not sure how well qualified I am, but I've done some production and planning work and I'd certainly be willing to learn. I'm a quick student.' She looked at Ogden thoughtfully. 'Could you use some help this spring? I don't think Lincoln will be needing me full time, say, starting some time in April.'

'That would be utterly fantastic!' Ogden said enthusiastically. 'By the way, how is old Link getting along? That was some dive he took, from what I read in the papers.'

'A lot better recently,' Cassie said. 'His face is still badly scarred, but plastic surgery will be able to take care of most of that as soon as he's recovered completely from the rest of his injuries.'

'Tch, tch, tch,' Ogden said gloomily, shaking his head. 'Poor old chap. He was always the one the rest of us lads looked up to. Seemed to have it all. But I dare say he'll be right as rain before long with such excellent nursing care.' His expression brightened. 'Can't have been an entirely ill wind, though, can it? It brought you back to us. I can't tell you how delighted I'll be to have your assistance. Martin Mayfield said he thought it would be just your cup of tea. By the way, how on earth did you manage to resist when the great Martin Mayfield asked you to marry him? There are usually women flocking around him in herds, waiting for a chance to bask in his magical aura. Poor Martin says he's still depressed over your refusal.'

So Ogden had looked into her love-life on his own. 'You're a snoop, Ogden,' Cassie said with an amused smile. 'I doubt if Martin's really still licking his wounds. Not with those herds of women around to distract him. They were the chief problem. I kept wanting to pick up my dad's old cattle prod and herd them all into a waiting trailer, to take to the auction barn. Some of them might have brought a pretty fair price, if the bidding was on the basis of previous experience.'

At that, Ogden roared with laughter. 'Ah, Cassie, you're a perfect Kate. We'll have a shrew that's not yet been tamed. I only hope that we can find a suitable Petruchio. One small slip, and no one will believe that he could do the job.'

'Thanks, I think,' Cassie said. 'When will you have the try-outs?'

'I'm waiting to hear when some other likely prospects can be here,' Ogden replied. 'I'll let you know the time if it's before the middle of April, although I doubt it will be. Meanwhile, brush up on your ability to go from tragedy to comedy in a flash. It's not the easiest thing in the world to go madder than a March hare one night and threaten to comb a chap's head with a three-legged stool the next.'

Cassie laughed. 'I'll do my best,' she replied.

She drove back towards Oak Hill, feeling elated. It was actually going to happen! Meanwhile, she had better do some serious studying of the various parts she might be required to either play or understudy in the little repertory company. Maybe, when Lincoln was a little better, he could read some of the other parts. It might be a good idea to give him something new and different to do, as well as make him feel a part of her new enterprise. She wouldn't want him to think that she was looking forward to leaving him, especially after what he had said today.

Now that she thought about it, Cassie doubted that Lincoln had anything as serious as marriage in mind so soon. He probably just felt grateful to her for helping him, and wanted to keep her near until he felt really well again. She certainly had no desire to leave him. It was wonderful to see him progressing, to feel the warmth of his beautiful smile. But she did want him to know that she was serious about going on to the stage, if only in a small way in Midvale, so that he would not jump to the conclusion that her willingness to stay with him meant that she was just waiting for a chance to become a permanent part of his life. He was very special, but there was still so much about him that she didn't know, didn't understand. Maybe she never would. In a few weeks, Lincoln might return to New York, fading from her life just like any other patient. Cassie bit her lip and blinked rapidly. That was a miserable thought. She would hate it if he went away and she never saw him again. She didn't want to think about that happening at all.

'Oh, stop borrowing trouble,' she muttered to herself. 'You're getting way ahead of yourself, as usual.' In the distance she could see the towering cedar trees marking the turn-off into the long, cedar-lined drive to Oak Hill. She looked at her watch. Still an hour until she was due back. She might as well stop and tell her parents the good news from Ogden and find out when she could bring Colleen over to see the spring calves.

'Does that mean you'll be coming here to stay?' Cassie's mother asked when she told her of her prospective job with the Shakespeare festival.

'Well, I'll be staying somewhere in the vicinity,' Cassie replied. Better not to say anything about Lincoln's desire to keep her with him, which would raise questions she was far from ready to answer. 'I promised Lincoln's little girl, Colleen, that I'd bring her over to see the baby animals some time soon. Are there some new calves yet?'

'Three on the ground and six more due any time,' her father reported. 'We can take her over to the Johnsons', too. They've got some of those miniature goats now. Cute as they come.'

'What's the little girl like?' asked Mrs Lewis. 'I heard her mother was a real beauty.'

'I expect she was,' Cassie replied, then told her parents for the first time of Colleen's handicap.

'Well, my goodness, she's not so badly off, is she?' her mother said. 'She'll get along just fine, if she has plenty of loving and some good firm discipline. It's awfully easy, though, for parents to forget the discipline when they've got a handicapped child. Seems they feel guilty, or something. My friend Alice Detweiler's daughter has a child like that, so I've seen some of the problems.'

'From what her nanny said, Colleen's already pretty good at exploiting her difficulties,' Cassie said, 'but all we have to do is entertain her for a while. I'll let you know before we come. I'd better go now, and rescue Lincoln from Pat Wanamaker's non-stop talking.'

Cassie retraced the short distance to the Oak Hill drive and turned in, eager to tell Lincoln her news, and curious about what his reaction would be. That, she thought, might give her some clue about what he had had in mind when he told her he was not going to let her go. There was a strange car in the courtyard formed by the now asphalted expanse between the mansion and the old carriage house. It was a low-slung, very expensive sports car. Just the sight of it sent a premonitory surge of anxiety rushing through Cassie, making her feel almost ill. Almost as if it were etched on that car, one name entered her mind. Tyler. Could that snake have actually come here? she wondered.

One look at Willton's face gave her the answer. He had been watching for her, and opened the door before she could do so herself.

'Mr Tyler is here,' he announced in grim tones. 'I tried to make him wait until you returned before he went to see Mr Snow, but he went right ahead anyway.'

'When did he get here? What does he want?' Cassie asked, hurrying towards the stairs.

'Only a few minutes ago,' Willton replied. 'I have no idea what he may want, although money is his usual reason for coming to Mr Snow when he's been away for a while. However, I doubt very much that it will do Mr Snow any good to see him.'

Cassie flung her hands out in a desperate gesture. 'What can I do?'

Willton took hold of her arm in an unusually familiar demonstration. 'Just be there, Miss Cassandra,' he said, his old voice quavering with emotion. 'Just be there.'

'Shall I go now?' asked Pat Wanamaker, who was hovering anxiously in the hall.

Cassie nodded and let herself into her own room as quietly as she could. The door into Lincoln's room was only partly closed, and she could plainly hear all that was being said.

'Come on, Link, old boy, no hard feelings,' Cassie heard Tyler say as she flung off her sweater and skirt and slipped into her nurses' uniform in record time. 'You know as well as I do that either one or both of us could have gone through that railing. I was just lucky. Of course ...'

At that point, Tyler lowered his voice. Cassie could not hear what he said, and, if Lincoln made any reply, she could not hear it. She went through the door, still fastening on her tiny nurses' cap. The change in Lincoln almost tore her heart out. He seemed to have shrunk and paled, as if some malevolent spirit had waved a wand of chilling evil over him. Tyler, on the other hand, looked as healthy as a horse, his face tanned from wherever he had been in the time since Lincoln had fallen. He looked up and gave Cassie a leering smile.

'Well, as I live and breathe, if it isn't Cassie Lewis!' he exclaimed. 'What a cute little nursie you've turned into. No wonder old Link's still hanging around in the sick-room.'

'I find the fact that you live and breathe very annoying, Tyler,' Cassie said coldly. 'Now, get out of here. I have some medical procedures to take care of.'

'I'll just bet you do,' Tyler replied. He stood up from the chair he had pulled up next to Lincoln's wheelchair and came towards her. Cassie could see that he had grown to be what most young women would consider quite a handsome man, with his dark hair and deep-set brown eyes. His nose and chin were not as severely pointed as they had been when he was a child and she had called him 'weasel face', but there was still an insolence about his expression that raised her hackles before he could even speak. 'I'll come back in a little while,' he said, stopping next to Cassie and giving her a suggestive wink. 'Maybe later I could show you a few tricks that I've learned since we were little kids. It's been a long time.'

'Not long enough,' Cassie said, giving him an icy stare. 'As for tricks, I know a couple that will have you singing soprano for the rest of what I hope will be a very short life.'

'Phew,' Tyler said. 'Not exactly friendly, are you?'

'Not at all,' Cassie said. 'Now get out. If you want to be useful, ask Willton to send Max up here on the double.'

'OK, little nursie,' Tyler said, and sauntered from the room.

The Lincoln that Cassie now turned to was staring straight ahead, his face expressionless. He seemed, she thought, to be lost completely in some other world. If only she knew what had really happened that terrible night when Lincoln had fallen. From what she had overheard Tyler say, they had definitely been having a physical tussle beforehand. Could it have been, as Tyler claimed, only an accident? Somehow, she found that hard to believe. Obviously, from Lincoln's reaction, there was more to it than that.

'I don't believe that the return of Tyler Spenser was just what the doctor ordered,' she muttered. She bent and peered into Lincoln's face, smoothing his hair back with her hand as she did so. 'Are you all right?' she asked him, hoping that he would snap out of his doldrums and respond. Instead, he gave his head the slightest of negative shakes, clenched his jaw, and closed his eyes. Dear lord, Cassie thought, her heart sinking. I hope we're not back to square one.

She wheeled Lincoln's chair to his bedside just as Max appeared to help him back into bed. Max took one look at Lincoln and then looked anxiously at Cassie. She shook her head and shrugged helplessly. Max frowned unhappily, then lifted Lincoln in his powerful arms and very gently laid him on his bed. 'There you go, boss,' he said in his deep voice. 'Just whistle when you want to get back to your chair.'

Cassie followed him to the hallway, feeling that he deserved some explanation for Lincoln's changed appearance, but Max had already met Tyler. He jerked his head back towards Lincoln's room.

'That have something to do with that creep in the fancy car?' he asked.

'Everything,' Cassie replied. 'What did he do to you already?'

'He didn't do anything. He came and told me that the cute little nursie said for me to get my black...you know what...up here on the double. I knew you didn't say that. One more crack like that, and he's going for a fast ride without his car.'

'You've got my blessing,' Cassie said drily. 'He's been on my list for years.'

She returned to find that Lincoln had lowered his bed and was lying flat on his back, his eyes closed, just as she had seen him the first day that she arrived. His hands were clenched and the muscles in his arms hard and unyielding.

'I think I'll give you a back rub before I try your blood-pressure,' Cassie said. 'It's probably over two hundred right now. Turn over, please.' When Lincoln did not move, she sighed. 'Lincoln, do I have to get those pillows out again?' He turned, giving Cassie some hope that he was not going back to being completely uncooperative again. She kneaded vigorously on the knotted muscles in his shoulders, then worked her way down his back. She had just lowered his pyjama bottoms to work on his lower back when Tyler came into the room, unannounced, carrying the dinner tray.

'Hey, that's some medical procedure,' he said insolently. 'I'll take some of that myself, after we have our dinner. I thought it might be kind of nice to have a little family get-together for old times' sake.'

Cassie stared at him. Was there no end to his insensitivity? 'I think your uncle has had all of the family get-togethers he can take for a while,' she said as calmly as she could manage. 'Just leave the tray.'

'Like hell I will,' Tyler sneered. 'I came a long way to see my uncle and I don't plan to share his company with some gold-digging little farm wench, either. Why don't you just pull up his pants and buzz off and eat with the rest of the servants?'

Before Cassie could reply, Lincoln turned over and sat up with more agility than she would have believed possible, given the huge cast still on his right leg. His jaw was clenched, and on his face was a look of pure hatred.

'Get out, Tyler,' he growled, 'and stay out. I'll see you after breakfast in the morning.'

Tyler stared back, his eyes narrowed, then shrugged and smiled a nasty smile. 'Sure. Anything you say. So you and the little nursie have a good thing going. Can't say that I blame you. I'll just mosey into Midvale and see how things are going in that mecca of boredom.'

Bastard, Cassie thought, turning quickly to help Lincoln. 'Hold it a minute,' she said, raising the bed so that he did not have to lie back down without support. His forehead was beaded with sweat already. 'Ribs hurt? Leg throbbing?' she asked.

Lincoln shook his head. 'No, they're all right,' he said, giving a deep, shuddering sigh as he leaned back against his pillows.

'Stubborn,' she retorted, knowing that he was not telling the truth. 'You try that kind of gymnastics for the first time in weeks and it's bound to hurt.' She brought a damp cloth and sat down beside him. He closed his eyes while she gently mopped his face, then opened them again and gave her a sad little smile.

'You're an angel, Cassie,' he said.

'Me? An angel?' Cassie shook her head. 'No one's ever accused me of that before.' She started to clean Lincoln's large, square-shaped hands with the cloth in preparation for dinner, but he caught her hands and held them tightly.

'I'm afraid I don't feel much like eating tonight,' he said. 'Would you mind leaving me alone for a while? I have some thinking to do.'

Cassie stared at him, her lower lip caught in her teeth. She wanted to say that she did mind very much, that she wanted to hold him and kiss the sadness from his smile and bring the light of happiness back into his eyes. She wished so much that he'd let her help with whatever he needed to think about, but she was afraid that he would only retreat from her if she did. It was better that he feel she was there for him when he needed her.

'All right,' she said slowly, letting him know that she was very reluctant. 'But promise me you'll tell me if you get hungry later. You really shouldn't skip an entire meal.'

'I promise,' Lincoln said soberly, then smiled a warm, loving smile that seemed to come from a man completely free of his other worries. He tugged gently on Cassie's hands, urging her towards him. 'Would you mind very much giving me another kiss before you go? I think I've squeezed all of the mileage out of that last one that I can.'

'Would I mind?' Cassie repeated hoarsely. It was almost as if he had read her mind. 'Of course I wouldn't mind,' she said, bending towards him. Then she let out a little gasp, for Lincoln, with both arms now free to hold her, took her in his arms and possessed her lips with a passionate intensity that sent her head reeling dizzily and her heart pounding erratically. His tongue thrust inside her mouth, devouring her, deep sounds of pleasure emanating from his throat as she let her own emotions run free in response. She cradled him, her hands caressing his silky-soft brown hair, lost in the sensation of being pressed so close against him that their bodies almost seemed to melt together. She wondered that it did not hurt, his arms held her so tightly. Perhaps, she thought, the joy for him was greater than the pain. She knew that, if she were the one with mending bones, Lincoln's arms around her would chase away all but the most severe agony. Never before had she had such a strong sense of being in the very centre of all of the happiness in her world, in a spot from which she had no desire ever to move away.

For several minutes, Lincoln continued his strong, possessive searching of Cassie's mouth, the tender, loving caresses of his hands that explored her body as she lay close against him. When, at last, he pulled his head away, his arms still held her, one hand knotted deep in her thick, red-gold hair.

'Thank you, angel,' he murmured against her ear, 'I think that now, I could face almost anything.' His arms released her, and Cassie slowly raised her head, shaken at the intensity of emotions she still felt. She had felt a strong attraction to him before, an affectionate warmth deep inside, but the longing she felt now was much stronger. The sense of oneness with him was now a physical desire that was almost overwhelming. She trembled as Lincoln gently caressed her cheek and smiled at her.

'That's the closest thing I know to a magic potion that makes the rest of this ugly world go away,' he said. 'Tell you what.' He looked at his watch. 'Why don't you bring me another dose at about ten o'clock, along with some soup and crackers? I always work better when I have a deadline to meet, and with an incentive like that I'm sure to do some of my best thinking in a long time.'

'A-all right,' Cassie agreed. It might be foolish to send her emotions to that fever pitch again, but the lure of Lincoln's smile was irresistible. She would do anything to keep him from sinking into that miserable sadness. Thank goodness, he seemed to have recovered quickly from the worst effects of his encounter with Tyler. Perhaps, after the initial shock, it had spurred him to confront something he had been avoiding. She smiled, then suddenly leaned forward and took Lincoln's face between her hands. 'Don't think too hard,' she said, kissing him again quickly.

Cassie picked up the dinner tray and carried it into her room, where she picked at some of the food, not having much desire to eat either. She felt weak from the slamming back and forth of her emotions from one extreme to the other. On the one hand was the absolute joy of being held and caressed in Lincoln's arms. On the other was a terrifying and growing hatred for Tyler. If only he would just go away again, like a bad dream! Whatever it was that Lincoln was going to think about, she hoped it included some plan to get rid of Tyler very quickly. For, like a lioness with a cub to protect, she knew that she could and would do anything necessary to keep Lincoln safe.

To pass the time, Cassie picked up the script of *Macbeth* that Ogden Warren had given her and began rereading the familiar words of Shakespeare. As never before, a chilling recognition gripped her as Lady Macbeth went slowly mad over her complicity in the murder of the king, trying in futile agony to wash the blood from her hands, while the guilt-ridden Macbeth moved on to his inevitable doom. No wonder, she thought with a new understanding, the plays of Shakespeare lived on, as fresh and new as the day they were written. No man had ever understood the intricacies of the human mind more completely, nor expressed them with such uncanny perceptiveness that everyone could recognise his or her bleakest thoughts and greatest joys in Shakespeare's words.

Cassie was still brooding from her new insight into the role of Lady Macbeth when she went downstairs to prepare Lincoln's soup for their ten o'clock appointment.

'Is Mr Snow not feeling any better?' Willton asked anxiously, peering at her sombre face.

Startled, Cassie stared at Willton for a moment, then laughed. 'Yes, I believe he is feeling better. He's been resting and wanted some soup brought at ten o'clock. I've been reading *Macbeth* since I may be playing the part of Lady Macbeth or understudying it this summer. That's why I look so gloomy.'

'You must be a method actor,' Willton said knowingly.

'Method in my madness?' Cassie asked with a grin.

At that, Willton actually laughed out loud. 'How delightful to have someone so literate about the house,' he said. 'Shall I bring the tray when the soup is ready?'

'No, I'll take it up,' Cassie replied quickly. It wouldn't do for Willton to appear just when she was giving Lincoln his promised next kiss.

She was thinking about that kiss with excited anticipation as she started towards the staircase. Just then, she heard the sound of the large outside door, opening and closing behind her. Wonderful, she thought grimly. Tyler returns. She did not turn her head when his footsteps hurried towards her.

'Time for a little bedtime snack?' he asked.

Cassie stopped. 'Not exactly,' she said. 'You got your uncle so upset before that he didn't feel like eating his dinner. He feels better now.'

Tyler smiled slyly. 'I'll bet you knew how to make him feel better, didn't you?'

'You're disgusting,' Cassie said, starting towards the staircase again.

'Wait a minute!' Tyler grabbed hold of Cassie's arm. 'I think it's time you and I had a little talk. I'm getting pretty damned tired of you talking like that to me. I'm going to be around here for a while, and I don't like employees mouthing off every chance they get. You'd better straighten up, little nursie.'

'Straighten up?' Cassie glared at him. 'I've been far nicer to you than you deserve, and you know it. Besides, I'm not your employee. If Lincoln has any complaints, he can tell me personally.' She caught her breath in a gasp as Tyler clamped his hand on her arm in a punishing grip. 'Let go of me, Tyler,' she warned.

Tyler ignored her. 'Give me that tray,' he said, wrenching it from her grasp with his other hand. He dragged her after him into the darkened salon, setting the tray down carelessly on the edge of a lamp table.

Then he jerked Cassie towards him, one arm enclosing her in a vicelike grip while his other hand took a tight hold of her hair behind her head. He bent so close that she could smell the liquor on his hot breath.

'Let me go!' Cassie demanded, feeling her pulse begin to pound. Tyler, she was sure as she looked into the dark, cruel blankness of his eyes, was capable of anything.

'Shut up,' Tyler replied, giving her hair a vicious jerk. 'You really are pretty,' he said, his eyes sweeping over her face. 'Too bad you have such a lousy temper. But I think I know exactly how to fix that. Little old Tyler's got a lot more going for him than that scarred-up old wreck upstairs. So why don't you just hold still for a minute and I'll show you what I mean?'

Cassie tried to squirm from his grasp, but Tyler yanked on her hair so hard that he almost dislocated her neck, at the same time planting his lips on hers, hard and vile-smelling. Cassie gritted her teeth, trying every move she could think of to free herself. It was obvious that Tyler had used this approach before, for he was very good at defending himself from her elbows and knees, at the same time thrusting his slimy tongue in between her lips with vulgar, slurping noises. At last, Cassie took a chance on opening her mouth, doing so and then quickly biting down on Tyler's tongue as hard as she could.

'You damned little bitch!' he swore, pulling his head back and wiping his mouth.

'Let me go, or I'll scream bloody murder,' Cassie rasped. 'I don't want to disturb Lincoln, but I won't stand for having you touch me.'

'Oh, yeah!' Tyler leered. 'I can see that you're getting hot. I can see it in your eyes. And you're right,

I do want to touch you.' He let go of Cassie's hair and, in one swift move, grabbed the front of her dress and ripped it open clear to her waist, managing to catch her bra and rip it in half at the same time. 'Wow! Look at that!' he cried, clutching at her breast.

For the split second that it took Tyler to tear her clothes, Cassie had stood immobilised in disbelief. But when his fingers dug cruelly into her flesh she screamed over and over and struck out at him with all of her strength, at last wrenching herself free. She clutched her clothing together and ran, screaming and sobbing, for the staircase, Tyler following behind her, laughing.

As she passed the brass gargoyle on the pedestal she abandoned the futile hold on her torn dress and grabbed the heavy object with both hands as she ran by on her way to the staircase. In two bounds she had covered half a dozen stairs. There she stopped, breathing heavily, and turned, the gargoyle raised over her head. Come on, Tyler, she thought, take one more step and I'll mash you like a bug!

CHAPTER FIVE

THERE was a crashing noise in the hall above her.

'Cassie, no!' Lincoln's voice commanded. 'My God!' he cried as Cassie turned to look up at him. 'Willton!' he bellowed. 'Cassie, get up here. Tyler, don't move,' he ordered in swift succession.

Cassie put down the gargoyle, clutched her dress together, and vaulted up the stairs. 'Lincoln, what are you thinking of?' she cried, for he had somehow got himself to the head of the stairs without the aid of crutches or his wheelchair and was standing there, holding on to the railing.

'You!' he snapped impatiently. 'Go on into your room and stay there until I call you. Now!' as Cassie hesitated.

Cassie reluctantly started for her room as Lincoln had ordered. Below, she heard Tyler whining, 'Hey, she was coming on to me, but she didn't like it when she got what she asked for.' Lincoln's reply to that was the most searing stream of profanity that Cassie had ever heard.

She paused by her door, listening to Lincoln ordering Willton to call Max, then bring him his briefcase. A few moments later she heard Max's heavy tread bounding up the stairs, and Lincoln said, 'Come on up, Tyler.' She slipped inside her door before she could be seen. Why, she wondered, did Lincoln want Willton to bring his briefcase? She was sure that Tyler had come for money, not love. Was Lincoln actually

82

going to give him some, after the havoc he had caused? It might be one way to get rid of him temporarily, but he would only come back again, whining and insulting and as disgusting as ever. Surely Tyler must be almost twenty-one by now, quite old enough to fend for himself. Why didn't Lincoln simply tell him to go away? What kind of hold did Tyler have on him?

Cassie was very tempted to listen by the door between her room and Lincoln's, but it seemed too dishonest a thing to do. After all, if Lincoln had wanted her to know exactly what he was going to do with Tyler, he would have invited her to come in. Maybe he would tell her later. Right now, she desperately wanted to take a shower and get rid of the feeling of Tyler's revolting lips on hers and his clammy hands clutching at her. He had not improved one iota from the horrid monster who had killed her baby bunny. If anything, he was worse, more dangerous now. What would he do to a woman who was alone, without a houseful of people to protect her?

Cassie shuddered at the thought, and then stepped into the soothing warmth of her shower, slathering on soap as if it could erase all of the sensations that had penetrated so deeply into her consciousness. "'Out, damned spot! Out, I say!'" she muttered the lines of Lady Macbeth, although the guilt was not hers. But, what if she had thrown the gargoyle? She thought of the possible consequences for a moment— Tyler lying in a pool of blood, his skull fractured— then shook her head. Not likely. He could too easily have deflected it. Besides, his head was probably as hard as a rock. She had seen too many crash victims who one would have thought could not possibly have survived, but who escaped with only minor injuries. It certainly wasn't to her credit that she had thought of dispatching Tyler, or at least slowing him down, but she doubted she was the first, nor would she be the last. If he didn't mend his ways, he was apt to be in more trouble than all of Uncle Lincoln's money could save him from one day.

There was still a sound of low voices in the next room when Cassie had finished her shower. She decided to abandon her nurses' garb for comfortable old jeans and a sweater, and had just slipped the sweater on when she heard the sound of Lincoln's door open and then close with a bang. A moment later, muffled by the distance, the huge outer door of Oak Hill slammed shut.

'Cassie!' Lincoln bellowed.

Was this, Cassie wondered, the new and improved Lincoln Snow? 'Coming, boss,' she yelled back, grabbing a comb and starting to run it through her damp hair. 'The call button broken?' she asked as she hurried into his room, still tugging at an unruly lock of hair.

Lincoln stared at her, his face grim at first, then suddenly a wide smile broke across his scarred face. 'No, it's not broken,' he answered, 'but I'm getting tired of playing hospital. How wonderful to see you in regular clothes. Are you really all right? Come here and let me look at you.' He held out his hand to her as Cassie came to his bedside.

'Of course I'm all right,' she replied, taking his hand and sitting down beside him on his bed. 'The question is, are you? How does your leg feel? Do you think we ought to have it X-rayed? You really shouldn't have put your weight on it so suddenly.'

'It feels fine. I took some of your children's pain-killer and that fixed the little twinge I had.' He carried Cassie's hand to his lips and kissed it lingeringly, then looked up at her from beneath his lashes. 'Tyler's gone,' he said. 'I thought you'd be happy to know that.'

Cassie looked at him thoughtfully. She was, of course, delighted that Tyler was out of the house, but she still was curious about why he had left. 'I'm glad,' she said. 'How did you persuade him to leave? He told me he was planning to stay a while.'

Lincoln returned her look levelly. 'He came for money,' he replied. 'I gave it to him, along with some sage advice, which he'll doubtless ignore. And before you tell me that I shouldn't have given him any money, I know it appears that way, but I have my reasons.'

'I assumed you must have,' Cassie replied, looking down and biting her lip. 'But it just means he'll come back again and again, and in between . . .' She raised her head and looked at Lincoln intently. 'It scares me to think of what he might do to some woman who was alone and defenceless. I'm sure that was neither the first, nor is it going to be the last time he's gotten rough with a woman.'

As if suddenly overcome by an intense pain, Lincoln bowed his head, his eyes closed. 'I know,' he said very softly. 'Generally, he prefers them willing, but there's always that chance. If there were anything I could legally do about it, I would.'

'I'm sure you would,' Cassie said quickly, wishing that she had not pursued a subject so obviously weighing heavily on Lincoln's conscience. She put her other hand on his, which was clenched tightly around hers, caressing it gently, not knowing quite what to say. 'You said you were tired of playing hospital,' she offered. 'We could get rid of most of this paraphernalia any time you want to.'

Lincoln raised his head, obviously willing to try to turn his attention to something more pleasant. 'I was thinking that earlier,' he said, looking around at the various white cabinets along the walls and the IV rack in the corner. 'I don't see why it can't all go and the regular furniture be put back. This used to be a very attractive room.'

'Did this used to be your room?' Cassie asked.

'No, mine was down the hall,' Lincoln replied, 'but I'd rather stay in this one. There's one of the features of this room that I'm not ready to give up.'

'Oh? What's that?' Cassie asked.

The remaining vestiges of sorrow again left Lincoln's face as he smiled at Cassie. 'Having you right next door,' he replied.

'I'm not sure I should encourage your being so dependent,' she teased gently. 'After all, in a few days you'll be going up and down the stairs and won't be using this room except to sleep in at night. You really won't need me here at all, once your cast is off. Even before that, there's not much excuse.'

'Do I need an excuse?' Lincoln asked, frowning. 'I told you I don't want you to go. It makes me feel good to have you here. Do you need more reason than that? It's not as if you were in a hurry to rush off and minister to some other poor sick soul. You can work on your plays just as well here as somewhere else, can't you?'

'Of course I can,' Cassie replied, immediately regretting having even mentioned the subject of her leaving. 'I was only teasing you.' She could tell by the way that an anxious look had reappeared so easily in Lincoln's eyes and in the deep, tense lines around them that he was very tired. She leaned over and caressed his hair back from his forehead. 'Did you ever get anything to eat?' she asked.

Lincoln shook his head and sighed. 'No, I guess I didn't. And there's something else I didn't get, either.' He raised his eyebrows at Cassie. 'Or did you forget?'

'No, I didn't forget,' she said, touching his lips with her forefinger, 'but I think I ought to feed you first. You're so tired and hungry that I doubt you're strong enough to survive another kiss like that last one.'

'Try me,' Lincoln suggested, pulling her towards him.

'No, no,' Cassie scolded, backing away. She looked at her watch. 'It's after eleven already. I'll run down and get something and be back in a few minutes. It wouldn't hurt for you to take a nap while I do.'

'Call Willton,' Lincoln suggested. 'He can get something for me.'

Cassie shook her head. 'Poor old fellow's probably sound asleep by now. He had a pretty traumatic day.'

'And you accused me of being stubborn,' Lincoln grumbled. 'All right, have it your way.'

Cassie went to the door and opened it. She was about to step through into the dimly lit hallway when suddenly a wave of panic overtook her. She started to tremble, her heart pounding. What if Tyler had sneaked back in, and was lurking in one of those shadows? She tried to shake off the dizzy, sick feeling and move forward, but could not make herself take even one step.

'Cassie?'

At the sound of Lincoln's voice, she turned her head and looked at him, trying unsuccessfully to smile at him with her frozen lips.

'Cassie, do you see that white button by the door-frame?' Lincoln asked, his voice suddenly loud and commanding. When she nodded he said firmly, 'Push it, then shut the door and come back here. Quickly.'

Suddenly mobilised, Cassie did as she was told, almost running the last few steps before she fell, sobbing, into Lincoln's outstretched arms. She clung to him, still trembling, trying to erase the vision of Tyler's hard, cruel face that seemed to have taken over her mind.

'Poor, brave little angel,' he murmured, holding her close and nuzzling his lips against her cheek. 'I thought you were taking that miserable experience far too lightly. Don't worry, my precious. I'll see that you're safe from now on.'

'H-how can you?' Cassie asked, raising her tearful face to look at him. It was only too easy to imagine Tyler coming at Lincoln, laughing that maniacal laugh of his as he flung him off that rooftop. 'Look what happened to you.'

Lincoln gave her a reproving look. 'Don't jump to any conclusions. Tyler did not throw me over the railing, if that's what you're thinking. However, I'll guarantee that what did happen will never happen again, thanks to you.' He smiled at Cassie's mystified expression. 'I'll admit that I haven't looked like any world-beater lately, but things will be different from now on. Believe me. Just as I promised, I got a lot of good thinking done earlier. Otherwise, I wouldn't have been able to decide so quickly exactly how to deal with Tyler tonight.'

'I don't understand——'

Cassie's complaint was interrupted by a tap on the door. 'Willton here, Mr Snow,' came the familiar voice.

'Come in, Willton,' Lincoln replied, pressing Cassie's head back against his shoulder. 'Delayed reaction,' he explained to Willton, patting Cassie's back comfortingly. 'She's very upset. Would you please bring us some soup and sandwiches and a stiff shot of brandy for both of us?'

'Certainly, sir,' Willton replied. Cassie heard his footsteps retreat a little way and then stop. 'Good heavens, sir,' Willton said then. 'You never had your dinner, did you? I'm terribly sorry. I completely——'

'That's all right,' Lincoln interrupted gently. 'I didn't feel like eating until just now anyway. It's been a difficult day for all of us.'

'Thank you, sir,' Willton said, then hurried from the room.

'He is the dearest person,' Cassie said, her voice muffled against Lincoln's shoulder. She raised her head, blinking away the last of her tears. 'You're pretty dear, yourself, Lincoln Snow,' she said. 'How did you know I was about to fall apart? I didn't even know it myself.'

'Watching you, I could almost feel what you were feeling,' Lincoln replied, dropping a little kiss on Cassie's cheek. 'Maybe that's because I love you so much.'

Cassie sat bolt upright and stared at him, scarcely able to believe what she had heard. 'Are—are you sure?' she stammered. 'A little while ago you only said you . . . you wanted me to stay because it made you feel good. When did you decide that ... that you love me?'

Lincoln smiled. 'Come back here,' he said, reaching out and pulling her close to him again. 'I'm not surprised that you're confused, but yes, I'm sure,' he said, caressing her hair as she nestled against him. 'Very sure. I thought perhaps I shouldn't tell you until you'd gotten used to the idea that I'm not some pitiful wreck who wouldn't even talk to you. It wasn't very long ago. But I decided that, given how disturbed you are by what you've been through tonight, you needed to know very definitely that I'm not just another man who lusts after your beautiful body. Remember that time that I found you by the roadside, crying over your poor old dog?'

Cassie nodded against his shoulder. 'Oh, yes. I remember that very well. I told you we still have the puppy you brought me, didn't I? You seemed to know just how I felt then, too. But that was so long ago. What does that have to do with now?'

'Everything,' Lincoln said, kissing her cheek. 'There was a special spark between us then, too, although I didn't recognise at the time what it meant. But I remember clearly that I wondered then why I felt your sorrow so deeply, and many times since then I've been haunted by the question of why I never could feel so completely a part of another person's experience as I did with you that day. It's an extraordinary feeling, that I wish with all my heart I'd understood sooner.' He sighed. 'I guess the time wasn't right. You were a sweet young girl, almost an old friend, who had suffered a terrible loss. I still thought of you as a child. After all, I was in my twenties, and you were only ... how old?'

'Fourteen,' Cassie replied with a sigh. 'I didn't think of you as an old man, though. I was head over heels in love with you after that. I thought it was just puppy love.'

Lincoln paused in his caressing of her hair. 'It probably was, and, then again, perhaps that was the beginning for both of us,' he said, his voice soft and warm. 'Of course, there's more to love than just feeling wonderful when you're with someone. There has to be mutual respect and understanding. It's only natural if you're still uncertain, and I don't want you to feel you need to say anything more just because I'm so sure of what I want.'

Cassie raised her head and looked deeply into Lincoln's clear hazel eyes. He did understand her, so very well. How could she help but love him? Still . . . She smiled and laid her hand against his cheek. 'You're right that I am still uncertain. There are so many things I don't understand, about both you and myself. So much has happened to you in the past dozen years that I don't know about. And I'm not sure about my own life, either. I've told you how I feel about the theatre, and there's a chance I might have a year-round job here, if the Shakespeare Festival goes well. That would be a dream come true for me.' She stopped and bit her lip, her forehead furrowed in a worried frown. Lincoln was studying her so seriously. She didn't want to hurt him, but she had to be honest.

'I'd never try to tie you down to a life you don't want, Cassie,' he said. 'But even if we decide to go our separate ways, I'll always love you. I don't think that will happen, though. I think that, eventually, when all of your questions are answered, you'll feel as strongly as I do that we belong together, for ever more. It may take some time for you to feel secure with me and respect me as a strong, solid person who can deal competently with all of the problems you already know I have, plus a few others you don't know about. Actually...' he smiled wryly '... I'm surprised you don't get up and run away when I tell you I'm planning to spend the rest of my life with you. I've been a lousy patient, rotten company most of the time, and I look like hell. I take it as a very good omen that you're at least willing to listen.'

Cassie smiled back at him. 'I'd be a fool not to. In spite of all of your imagined faults, I still see the man I saw when I was fourteen, a man who's warm and kind and understanding and who feels things very deeply and isn't ashamed to show it. I think that was what drew me to you most, in the first place. My father is such an unemotional person, on the surface at least. I love him, of course, but I could never be happy with a man like that. Maybe that's why I love Shakespeare. His characters are so passionate.'

'Which sometimes leads to their ruin,' Lincoln said, a slightly harsh undertone to his voice. 'It has to be balanced with reason. Something I've not always been able to do.'

'Neither have I,' Cassie said with a sigh. 'Sometimes reason just doesn't work. I found that out when I worked in the hospital. No matter how calm and detached I tried to be, sometimes I'd be an emotional wreck at the end of my shift. I knew I couldn't keep doing that indefinitely.'

'And then you came here and got put through the wringer again,' Lincoln said. He pulled Cassie back against his shoulder again and laid his cheek against

her hair. 'I saw you that very first time you came into
my room. After you'd looked at me, you sat over in
that chair and cried your lovely eyes out. I'm sorry
you had to go through that, but I think you saved my
sanity. I felt so trapped in my own spiral of misery.
Then, suddenly, there you were, that same little girl
who lost her dog, still crying, this time over me. I
could feel your sorrow more deeply than my own, and
from that moment on I began to feel more and more
that you were a part of me that I must never lose
again. I wanted to protect you from any kind of unhappiness. But then,' he sighed heavily, 'the rest of
the world doesn't always co-operate, does it? Are you
feeling better now, or have I only added to your
problems?'

'By no means,' Cassie replied. 'I feel as if I'm
floating in a kind of wonderful dream.' She closed
her eyes. Nestled in Lincoln's strong arms, she felt
perfectly safe and secure. It was amazing, how similar
their feelings towards each other were. But was this
truly a love that would last forever? She needed to be
perfectly sure, for to tell Lincoln that she loved him
and later deny it would break his heart, and she could
never bear to hurt him like that.

A sharp tap on the door announced Willton's
return.

'Come on in, Willton,' Lincoln called.

'I'm sorry it took so long, sir,' Willton said, crossing
the room with a loaded tray, 'but Mrs Comstock insisted on making some fresh biscuits to go with the
chicken soup, and I believe someone filched the
brandy that was in the liquor cabinet. I had to go to
the cellar and get some from the reserve.'

'The soup smells wonderful,' Cassie said, raising her head as Willton set the tray on Lincoln's bedside table. 'I didn't know I was so hungry.' She caught Willton smiling at her benevolently and blushed furiously at the realisation of what he must think at the sight of her lying on Lincoln's bed, in Lincoln's arms.

'Don't be embarrassed, Miss Cassandra,' Willton said understandingly. 'It's a most pleasant sight, I assure you. If you need anything else, just ring.'

As Willton went out of the door, Lincoln murmured very softly in Cassie's ear, 'I wonder if he includes contraceptive devices in that offer? When I get this cast off, I'll have to check that out.'

For a moment, Cassie could not believe her ears. She jerked herself to a sitting position, frowning, then caught the twinkle in Lincoln's eyes and smiled a little uncomfortably. 'If I know Willton, he'd manage to do it without batting an eyelid,' she said, trying to sound casual. Lincoln had caught her completely off guard, switching from a rather abstract discussion of love to a much more concrete subject. It was doubtless realistic, given the way they responded to each other, but just the mention of it made her feel extremely vulnerable.

Lincoln picked up his bowl of soup and began to eat. 'Mmm, good soup.' He glanced at Cassie, who was eyeing him anxiously. 'What's the matter?'

'Oh, nothing. Nothing at all,' she replied, looking quickly away.

'Cassie, look at me,' Lincoln ordered. 'Is there something you want to tell me?'

Cassie shook her head. 'No, no. I was just curious. Who's the lucky girl?' Her cheeks turned pink as Lincoln suddenly roared at her.

'Cassie! Don't turn devious on me all of a sudden. Are you trying to tell me that you're a virgin and want to stay that way until you're married? If any other woman your age told me that I wouldn't believe it, but if you do, I will.'

For a moment, Cassie was speechless. Could Lincoln actually read her mind? 'You will? Why?' she asked. 'Do you think I'm strange?'

'I already told you I did,' Lincoln replied, grinning as Cassie glared at him across the large buttermilk biscuit she had held poised in front of her mouth for several minutes. 'You haven't answered my question. You seem very uncomfortable, discussing sex with me. I wouldn't have mentioned it at all, except that I've already made it clear that I have marriage as a goal, not a fling or a one-night stand. Given the way a kiss sets both of us on fire, I thought we ought to get the topic out in the open. After all, as a nurse, you've already seen all of me that there is to see, so what's the problem?'

'It's not the same thing,' Cassie replied, looking down. 'At least, it's not supposed to be.' She felt her cheeks grow warm again, and that made her feel cross and stupid. She took a deep breath and looked back at Lincoln. 'I guess I am uncomfortable about it, because I have a strong desire to have sex with you, more than I've ever had before with any man. Yes, I'm a virgin. No, I don't necessarily have to wait to get married. But I do have to be very sure of how I feel, and know that I do *want* to get married. There. Are you satisfied now?'

Lincoln gave her a sideways look. 'I don't believe satisfied is quite the word,' he said drily, 'but I do appreciate your being forthright about it. I shall try to keep my passions under control for a while longer. If you'll do the same.'

'Of course,' Cassie agreed. 'I'm not the kind to lead a man on and then slam the door in his face.'

In only a few more minutes, their midnight supper was finished. Cassie set the brandy snifters on the table, then carried the tray to the top of a cabinet. 'Perhaps we had better drink to a decorous goodnight kiss,' she suggested. 'I wish you hadn't brought up the subject of sex. Now it's preying on my mind.'

'Yours too? I've been having the same problem, but I don't mind it a bit. Of all the things that could be preying on my mind right now, that's the most pleasant.' Lincoln smiled and raised his glass. 'To decorous goodnight kisses,' he said, 'for everyone except us.' He took a sip of his brandy, then set his glass down and held out his arms towards Cassie. 'Come here, lovely creature,' he said. 'I want that kiss you promised me what seems like a hundred years ago now. The one that I was too weak and hungry to survive.'

'Is that...reasonable?' Cassie asked, feeling a great surge of longing to be in Lincoln's arms.

'Perfectly,' Lincoln replied. 'I want you to know that you can trust me, no matter how aroused I might be.'

'But you still have that cast on,' she whispered hoarsely, setting her brandy down and moving closer. The loving look in Lincoln's eyes, the gentle curve of his lips as he smiled, attracted her like a magnet. She

FREE GIFTS!

FREE BOOKS!

Play

CASINO JUBILEE

"Match'n Scratch" Game

PEEL OFF LABEL

PLACE LABEL INSIDE

CLAIM UP TO
4 <u>FREE</u> BOOKS,
A <u>FREE</u> VICTORIAN
PICTURE FRAME AND A
SURPRISE GIFT!

See inside

NO RISK, NO OBLIGATION TO BUY... NOW OR EVER!

CASINO JUBILEE
"Match'n Scratch" Game

Here's how to play:

1. Peel off label from front cover. Place it in space provided at right. With a coin, carefully scratch off the silver box. This makes you eligible to receive one or more free books, and possibly other gifts, depending upon what is revealed beneath the scratch-off area.

2. You'll receive brand-new Harlequin Romance® novels. When you return this card, we'll rush you the books and gifts you qualify for ABSOLUTELY FREE!

3. If we don't hear from you, every month we'll send you 6 additional novels to read and enjoy. You can return them and owe nothing but if you decide to keep them, you'll pay only $2.47* per book, a saving of 28¢ each off the cover price. There is *no* extra charge for postage and handling. There are *no* hidden extras.

4. When you join the Harlequin Reader Service®, you'll get our subscribers-only newsletter, as well as additional free gifts from time to time just for being a subscriber!

5. You must be completely satisfied. You may cancel at any time simply by sending us a note or a shipping statement marked "cancel" or returning any shipment to us at our cost.

YOURS FREE!

This lovely Victorian pewter-finish miniature is perfect for displaying a treasured photograph and it's yours absolutely free — when you accept our no-risk offer!

*Terms and prices subject to change without notice. Sales tax applicable in NY.

CASINO JUBILEE
"Match'n Scratch" Game

CHECK CLAIM CHART BELOW FOR YOUR FREE GIFTS!

YES! I have placed my label from the front cover in the space provided above and scratched off the silver box. Please send me all the gifts for which I qualify. I understand I am under no obligation to purchase any books, as explained on the opposite page.

(U-H-R-09/91) 116 CIH ADEY

Name

Address   Apt.

City   State   Zip

▼ DETACH AND MAIL CARD TODAY! ▼

HARLEQUIN "NO RISK" GUARANTEE

- You're not required to buy a single book — ever!
- You must be completely satisfied or you may cancel at any time simply by sending us a note or a shipping statement marked "cancel" or by returning any shipment to us at our cost. Either way, you will receive no more books; you'll have no obligation to buy.
- The free book(s) and gift(s) you claimed on the "Casino Jubilee" offer remains yours to keep no matter what you decide.

▲ DETACH AND MAIL CARD TODAY! ▲

BUSINESS REPLY MAIL
FIRST CLASS MAIL   PERMIT NO. 717   BUFFALO, NY

POSTAGE WILL BE PAID BY ADDRESSEE

HARLEQUIN READER SERVICE
3010 WALDEN AVE
PO BOX 1867
BUFFALO NY 14240-9952

NO POSTAGE
NECESSARY
IF MAILED
IN THE
UNITED STATES

tucked her hands behind Lincoln's shoulders and let him pull her towards him.

'It wouldn't stop me,' he said softly. 'Nothing would, except my desire to do nothing that you wouldn't want me to.' His eyes were glowing with that luminous warmth that destroyed the last vestiges of Cassie's resistance.

Her heart was beating so hard and fast that she could count its trembling pulses as their lips met. With a deep groan of contentment, Lincoln folded his arms around her. His kisses moved across her mouth in delicate little nibbles, like a connoisseur taking a first taste of a fine glass of wine. 'Heavenly. So perfect,' he murmured against the corner of Cassie's mouth, as if those had been his thoughts. He shifted so that Cassie was cradled in the curve of his shoulder, her head beside his on the pillow. 'Comfortable?' he asked.

'Mmm-hmm,' she replied, smiling. And contented, and happy, she thought, her hand behind Lincoln's neck caressing through his hair, now so silky and vital. If only this one room were all there were to the world, she would not mind in the least. Lincoln was lying perfectly still, his eyes holding hers, as if he were trying to let her see the truth of her mother's old dictum, that she could search to the bottom of his soul and would find nothing there but kindness and love for her. At last he smiled and closed his eyes, his mouth finding hers again, this time with an ever-increasing passion. His tongue teased along the line of her lips, waiting until she opened her mouth and met his tongue with hers to plunge inside, his own mouth covering hers, dominating firmly but gently. Cassie heard herself make a soft little sound of pleasure, and felt her skin responding with a tingling excitement that made the pressure of Lincoln's hands, now moving across her back beneath her sweater, turn into messages of desire that coursed through her with an increasing urgency. She knew that Lincoln's desire must be as strong as hers, for all at once he pulled his head back and held very still. Taking her cue, she stopped her own explorations beneath his pyjama top and tilted her head back to look at him. The dark, unbridled passion that she saw there startled her, but Lincoln seemed to recognise her uneasiness immediately.

'I'm all right. Don't worry,' he said, quickly giving Cassie a kiss on the tip of her nose. He took a deep breath. 'No woman's ever affected me quite as deeply as you can with just a kiss,' he said. He smiled crookedly. 'But I'm not complaining.'

'Maybe it's only because you've been deprived for so long,' Cassie suggested.

Lincoln shook his head. 'That's not it. I've been deprived before. It's you, my angel.' He gathered Cassie close again and then reached behind her and found the button which lowered the bed. 'Don't panic,' he whispered in her ear. 'I'm about to try to convince you that I'll be your idea of perfect husband.' When the bed was flat, he again reached beneath Cassie's sweater, this time unfastening her bra.

'Can I panic now?' Cassie asked, looking at him anxiously. 'I don't think I can take much more, either.'

Lincoln chuckled and levered himself away from her a little way. 'Just turn over on to your tummy,' he said, 'and pull your sweater up a little. I think I owe you one of those back-rubs that you'd walk across hot coals for. Unfasten your jeans, too, if you want me to get the lower part.'

Cassie hesitated, then smiled. 'All right,' she said, 'but you behave yourself.' She quickly sat up and unfastened her jeans, then flipped on to her stomach.

'Yes, ma'am. Just close your eyes, now, and relax,' Lincoln said in a seductively soft voice, beginning to squeeze the base of Cassie's neck. 'Pretend you're floating on a cloud.'

'Oooh, heavenly,' she murmured. 'Mmmm. That feels so good.' She sighed, letting her mind go blank, so that all the soothing warmth of Lincoln's hand could take over her consciousness. She could feel the tension drain from her body until she felt as if she really were floating on her own personal cloud, sinking into its softness, drifting along, and then . . . drifting off to sleep.

CHAPTER SIX

THE smell of the coffee on the tray that Cassie was carrying up the stairs seemed to be getting stronger and stronger. She looked down and was amazed to see that the tray was getting bigger and bigger, and was covered with dozens of cups of steaming coffee. Then, suddenly, she became aware that she was not carrying a tray at all, but was still lying in bed. What a vivid dream! But why was she still smelling coffee? She opened her eyes. Sitting directly in front of her in his wheelchair, holding a cup of coffee out in her direction, was Lincoln.

'Good morning, sleepyhead,' he said, grinning at her mischievously. 'Ready for some coffee?'

Cassie stared at him, then pushed herself up and looked around. 'I'm still here,' she said vaguely. 'Why didn't you . . . ?' She shook her head, then leaned over and took the cup from Lincoln. 'I didn't mean to fall asleep,' she muttered. 'I really didn't.' She took a large swallow of her coffee, at the same time noticing that Lincoln looked very pleased with himself. 'Why do I have the feeling that I was set up?' she asked.

'I wouldn't say you were exactly set up,' Lincoln answered, his eyes still twinkling, 'but I thought you might fall asleep if I rubbed your back. It was the only way I could think of to get you to sleep with me, especially in that hospital bed. I've already given orders to get rid of the thing today, and I think I've persuaded the doctor to take the cast off of my leg tomorrow. I've had enough of being an invalid. I want to be able to move around and do things. It's time Colleen had a father again.'

'It certainly is,' Cassie agreed. 'But I don't see how you got out of bed and into your chair alone without waking me. I didn't hear a thing.' She frowned. 'How many people came in and saw me in here? I don't want anyone thinking I've decided to become your live-in playmate so I don't have to leave now that my nursing duties are about over.'

'Only Willton saw you,' Lincoln said soothingly. 'And he would never think that. I slipped out of bed and found that I could put enough weight on my right leg to make it to my crutches. After that, I rang for Willton and went out in the hall and tried walking up and down. It was no problem, so I used the telephone out there to call Dr Norton. I couldn't manage carrying the coffee with those blasted crutches, though, so Willton saw you when he brought that in. I told him you were exhausted and fell asleep, and I didn't want to wake you to move you. You obviously were exhausted. You hardly moved all night.'

'I guess I must have been,' Cassie agreed, amazed at Lincoln's report. 'You look as though you slept like a log yourself. I don't see how you managed, with two people in this skinny bed. I should think you'd have been miserably uncomfortable.'

Lincoln shook his head, smiling that warm, glowing smile that set Cassie's still somewhat groggy head to spinning. 'I've never been more comfortable,' he replied. 'Most of the time I slept very well, and, when I did wake up and saw you there beside me, it was like finding a beautiful dream had come true.'

Cassie wrinkled her nose at him, trying to regain her equilibrium. 'Lincoln Snow, I think you must have kissed the Blarney stone at some time in your life,' she said. 'Not that I mind hearing such things, but you'll have me spoiled rotten if I ever get to believing them.'

'I doubt if you could be spoiled,' Lincoln said with another warm smile, 'but I'd love to try. You should have someone to fuss over you and take care of you for a change. And bring you little presents, and rub your back.'

Cassie felt her cheeks grow warm with pleasure. 'You do know how to tempt a girl, don't you?' she murmured, looking down into her coffee-cup. She had better be careful, or she would be saying yes to anything that Lincoln suggested! She finished her coffee and looked back at Lincoln. 'I'd better go and take a shower and get dressed. Is Willton going to be bringing breakfast?'

'No,' Lincoln replied, with a firm shake of his head. 'No more of this sick-room. I've had enough. After you're dressed, we'll go downstairs for breakfast. And when I say dressed, I mean in some regular clothes. You look adorable in your uniform, but I've had enough of that, too. I'm going to have Willton find me something to put on besides a bathrobe and one-legged pyjama bottoms.'

'Terrific,' Cassie replied. 'I'm as tired of that uniform as you are. I'll have to go home later and get some more clothes. I didn't bring much with me.' And, she thought, she would have to try to explain to her parents why she was going to be staying on at Oak Hill if Lincoln no longer needed her as a nurse. That would take some ingenuity!

Back in her own room, Cassie quickly stripped for her shower. She took a moment to eye herself critically in the long mirror on the bathroom door. Not too bad, she decided, but definitely not voluptuous. She'd always been a little on the thin side. Lincoln would have got a brief look at her when she ran up the stairs last night, but he had probably been too distracted to notice very much. Maybe, some day soon, if things went well ... Cassie frowned reprovingly at her own image and quickly turned on the shower. Lincoln and sex were definitely getting very closely linked in her mind. If she hadn't been so exhausted last night, there was no telling what might have happened! She had better get her mind on something else. Perhaps she should rehearse some of Kate's speeches from *The Taming of the Shrew*. Those she made before she capitulated to Petruchio's persuasive courting.

When Cassie returned to Lincoln's room, wearing her favourite light blue trousers and a sweater with a pattern of little ducks and a blue sky with fleecy clouds around the yoke, she found that Lincoln was sitting on the edge of his bed, already wearing a gold-coloured sweater and brightly striped, low-cut briefs. Seeing his broad, masculine shoulders and nicely rounded bottom, coupled with the welcoming smile he gave her, quickly undid Cassie's attempts at self-discipline. She resolutely turned her attention to Willton, who was applying the scissors to one leg of some tan trousers.

'It does seem to me,' she said, eyeing the operation critically, 'that if the cast is coming off tomorrow you could have stayed with the pyjama bottoms one more day instead of wrecking a good pair of trousers.'

'I thought about that,' Lincoln said, 'but I think I must have hit some kind of a limit last night. I may never wear pyjamas again. I hate the damned things.'

'I think that will do it, sir,' Willton said. He bent and slid the trousers on to Lincoln's legs, and Cassie quickly hurried to Lincoln's side so that he could lean on her if he needed while he fastened them.

'I can stand up perfectly well,' Lincoln said, reading her intentions and giving her a defiant glance. He fastened his trousers and pulled down his sweater. 'There. If it weren't for a face like a patchwork quilt and one leg like a tree-stump, I'd look almost human.' He looked at Cassie, as if expecting confirmation.

'I'd say you look terrific right now,' she said, for to her he did and she was sure it would be useless to say otherwise, as easily as Lincoln read her thoughts these days.

'You could use a haircut, sir,' Willton suggested. 'I could send for a barber, if you'd like.'

Lincoln shook his head. 'I don't believe I'll have it cut for a while. I've had enough of looking like Mr Wall Street.' He cocked a questioning eyebrow at Cassie. 'What's your preference in men's hairstyles? Short or long?'

Cassie could see Willton look back and forth between her and Lincoln in that quick, surreptitious way of his, obviously putting together the information that she and Lincoln were not in a patient-nurse relationship any more. 'Anything you like,' she said with a shrug. 'You may need it shaped a little pretty soon, since it's all the same length, or you'll look like a haystack.'

Lincoln smiled at that, but made no reply. 'Get me my crutches, please, Willton,' he said, nodding towards the corner where they were propped.

'Yes, sir,' Willton said. 'Shall I send for Mr Max?'

'No, I'll manage without him,' Lincoln replied, tucking the crutches under his arms as Willton handed them to him.

'You aren't seriously thinking of going down those stairs alone, are you?' Cassie demanded, mentally picturing Lincoln tumbling head over heels down the long flight.

'I am not only thinking of it, I am going to do it,' Lincoln replied, starting towards the door.

'Lincoln, that's crazy,' Cassie said, hurrying after him and clutching at his arm. Something had definitely happened to him last night, during his hours of meditation or whatever they had been. He had obviously become very determined on several fronts, but he was not necessarily being reasonable. 'If you fall, you could be right back in that stupid hospital bed again,' she pointed out.

'I will not fall,' Lincoln said. 'Let go.' He impatiently shook her hand off. 'I've figured out how to do it, so just stand aside.' He frowned at both Cassie and Willton, who were looking first at him and then at each other anxiously. 'Neither of you has any imagination,' he said. 'Just watch me.' He swung along until he got to the top of the long staircase, then carefully lowered himself to sit on the top step and handed his crutches to Willton. Then, one step at a time, he let himself down, sitting down, until he was a little over halfway down. He stood back up, took a crutch, and went down the rest of the way using the banister to help him. 'I'll do a few more steps standing up each time,' he announced with a self-satisfied smile, to Cassie and Willton, who were now only interested onlookers. 'That way, I can build up both my arms and leg and get down safely.' He gave Cassie a reproving look. 'That will teach you to doubt me,' he said.

'Yes, sir,' Cassie said meekly. Apparently Lincoln had not lost all of his common sense, as she had feared, but had become very determined to get back to a normal life as quickly as possible. That idea was reinforced when they got near to the dining-room, and Colleen suddenly came swinging through the doorway on her own little crutches. The child stopped, staring.

'Daddy!' she cried, bursting into tears. 'You're still broken!'

Lincoln froze, his previously happy look turning so thoroughly miserable that Cassie leaped into the breach. 'Not for much longer, Colleen,' she said. 'But your daddy thought you'd like to see that big, funny cast on his leg before they take it off tomorrow.' She had got so used to the scars on Lincoln's face that she had forgotten how much they, too, might shock Colleen.

'But his face is all ugly,' Colleen wailed.

'Oh, dear me,' Mrs Lindstrom said, wringing her hands helplessly.

'Colleen,' Cassie said, quickly crouching down in front of her, 'listen to me. Those are scars that will go away after a while. Do you remember what I told you about looking into a person's eyes?'

Colleen sobbed and nodded.

'All right, then, you go and sit on your daddy's lap and look into his eyes. You'll see that he's just as beautiful inside as ever.' She pulled a Kleenex from her pocket and dabbed at Colleen's tears. 'Come on, don't cry or your daddy will feel bad. He's waited so long to see you again. He needs a hug and a kiss from you to make him feel better.'

Colleen reluctantly followed Lincoln into the dining-room and let Cassie put her on his lap. She looked dubiously into Lincoln's face, her little mouth puckered in worry. Lincoln, Cassie noted, looked every bit as anxious as Colleen. If only he would take the initiative and give her a big hug and a smile, it might help. Instead, he said rather stiffly, 'What was that I heard about looking into my eyes?'

'Your nurse told me you could tell if someone was pretty that way,' Colleen replied, squinting and looking carefully at Lincoln.

Lincoln cast a questioning glance at Cassie, who quickly got up and whispered the story into Lincoln's ear, so that she could also tell him of Colleen's touching worry about her appearance that had pre-cipitated her little tale.

'I see,' Lincoln said gravely. He turned his at-tention back to Colleen, his face softening as he brushed her coppery curls back from her forehead. At last, he smiled at her and asked, 'Well, how am I doing? Do I look better inside than I do outside?'

Colleen nodded. 'Lots better,' she said. She looked hopefully at Lincoln. 'Do I?'

'Oh, lord,' Lincoln said, suddenly holding Colleen tightly and kissing her soft little cheek. 'Sweetheart,' he said huskily, 'you look beautiful both inside and out. No daddy ever had a more adorable little girl.' He rubbed his cheek against her beautiful curls, and Cassie could tell by the way he was blinking rapidly that Colleen's innocent question had touched him deeply. Apparently, Cassie thought, he hadn't known how aware Colleen already was of the fact that she was different, and how worried the little girl was about it. But then, Willton had told her that Lincoln had not spent a great deal of time with the child. Perhaps it was time that he got to know his own daughter better!

Cassie also saw the truth of Mrs Lindstrom's statement that Colleen wrapped Lincoln around her little finger. He seemed not to have caught the concept of discipline, she mused, as Colleen loudly demanded some new toys because she hadn't had any in so long.

'I'll find you some when I go to get my cast off tomorrow,' Lincoln promised without batting an eyelid. 'What would you like?' He also did nothing when Colleen tried to interrupt a brief conversation that Cassie and Lincoln were having about the history of Oak Hill. She yelled, 'Daddy!' several times, to which he responded, 'Just a minute, sweetheart.' Then she deliberately spilled her milk glass. When Mrs Lindstrom scolded her, quite mildly, Cassie thought, Lincoln said calmly that he was sure it was an accident. After that, Colleen tilted her little chin up and gave Mrs Lindstrom a look that plainly said, 'So there, too!'

It was all that Cassie could do to keep quiet about that. What was Lincoln trying to do? Raise another Tyler Spenser?

After breakfast, Lincoln told Colleen that he would come to the nursery later and see her. 'Let's take a little walk outside,' he suggested to Cassie when she had gone. 'I think we need to have a little talk.

'Good idea,' Cassie agreed, for she had decided that she and Lincoln had better have a discussion about child psychology. If Lincoln had marriage in mind, she might as well let him know right away that children were important to her, and a father who knew how to be firm when it was required was equally important.

They went out to the terrace, and then walked slowly along the path by the pond, admiring the tulip beds that Max had brought back to a sparkling, weed-free order. 'All right,' Lincoln said finally, 'out with it. You looked daggers at me several times at breakfast, and I could almost hear you muttering to yourself, ''he's a lousy father''. We'd better get such things up front right now.'

'My sentiments exactly,' Cassie said, relieved that Lincoln was at least willing to discuss the problem. 'The only reason I kept my mouth shut this morning was that I don't think it's a good idea to have two people working at cross purposes in front of a child. Of course, I may be jumping to the wrong conclusions. Maybe you were being especially lenient with Colleen because you hadn't seen her in so long.'

'You thought I was too lenient?'

'I just said that I did.'

'Why? Because I didn't scold her for spilling her milk?' Lincoln frowned at Cassie. 'Are you sure it wasn't an accident?'

'Positive. Mrs Lindstrom saw her, too. If you want to make life impossible for Mrs Lindstrom, just keep countermanding when she tries to discipline Colleen.'

'Well, I suppose you have a point,' Lincoln said, his mouth twisted in obvious displeasure. 'I do hate to see Colleen hurt, though, just because she's not as well co-ordinated as other children.'

'I wouldn't want that, either,' Cassie replied, 'but she's very bright and already knows how to use her disability to take advantage of a situation. But, since you asked, that wasn't the only thing that bothered me. She doesn't have to be well co-ordinated to learn not to interrupt, and she shouldn't have the idea that all she has to do to get something is say "gimme". I can't picture you running into the jewellers tomorrow to buy me a few diamonds just because I told you I hadn't had any in a long time.'

Lincoln shrugged. 'I might do that.'

'Oh, for heaven's sake, Lincoln, that would be stupid!' Cassie said impatiently. 'You should be smart enough to see that it turns something special into something completely meaningless. It's one thing to be soft-hearted and another to be soft-headed. Colleen's trying to tell you the only way she knows how that she needs love and attention.'

'I know she does,' Lincoln said with a heavy sigh. 'You aren't telling me anything I don't already know.' He stopped and sat down on a garden bench that overlooked the pond from beneath a huge oak tree, staring into the distance with a sad, withdrawn look that reminded Cassie of the look he had had on his face when she first saw him a few weeks before. 'I've tried to get more involved in her upbringing several times,' he said slowly, 'but every time I do she eventually misbehaves and I find myself turning away from doing what I know should be done.'

'Turning away?' Cassie frowned. 'Lincoln, I hate to sound so terribly practical, but you're going to have to stop doing that. I don't think you're a lousy father yet, but I do think you need to start acting like a good one. I can't see myself raising a family with a man who can't take a good firm line with the children when it needs to be done. Children are very important to me. If you want to convince me that you're the man I should marry, I need to see that you can handle Colleen. I know she's not my child, but . . .' She stopped, arrested by the most haunted look she had yet seen on Lincoln's face. 'Lincoln,' she whispered. 'What is it?'

'She's not my child, either,' he replied.

CHAPTER SEVEN

'SHE'S not . . . your child?' Cassie repeated Lincoln's words as a question, her voice hoarse as she forced the words past the knot of tears that had formed in her throat. 'Then whose . . .?' She stopped herself before she could blunder further. Lincoln would tell her, she was sure, when he could. At the moment, she could see that he was fighting his own strong emotions, trying to get himself in control before he spoke again. When he finally spoke, his face was blanked of any emotion, but his voice was harsh with strain.

'I guess this is as good a time as any to tell you the whole story,' he said. 'There's nothing I can do to make it any more pleasant for either of us.' He looked down and picked up one of Cassie's hands, tracing the delicate line of veins with his other forefinger. 'I suppose the best place to begin is at the beginning,' he said, at last looking back at Cassie, 'but now I'm not so sure exactly when that was. Maybe it was that day by the roadside, when I found you there, your hair glistening red in the sunlight, hiding a face I knew was sweet and wet with tears. Maybe that was why, when I met Magda, whose hair was red, too, like Colleen's, I was immediately attracted to her. She was beautiful, too, and vivacious, and very wealthy. Just to find that she was apparently attracted to me, too, was flattering. I used to be fairly good-looking, but I'd never put much effort into a playboy image, and those were the men who usually flocked around Magda. Maybe I was a novelty to her, I don't know. Anyway, to cut a long story short, we followed our mutual attraction where it led, first to bed and then to the altar. I knew there were things about her that I didn't like very well, especially her drinking, but there were plenty of more favourable things, not the least of which was her passionate nature. She fussed over me and played at being the perfect wife so well that I was completely deceived. In fact...' Lincoln paused and stared into space '...she deceived me until the day she died,' he finally concluded. 'We travelled quite a bit. One of our trips, the summer after we were married, was to Florida, to visit my parents. Tyler was there then, of course, and my two youngest sisters. He was only fourteen, but already causing my parents a lot of grief. He'd "borrowed" a couple of fancy cars, and wrecked one of them, just for fun. He'd gotten one of his classmates pregnant. My parents had sought professional help for him several times, but nothing seemed to work. My mother admitted that he was completely out of control.

'When we got home, I was rather surprised that Magda kept remarking on what a quote "cute little guy" unquote Tyler was.'

'Oh, lord,' Cassie breathed, a sick knot in her stomach joining the lump in her throat.

Lincoln raised his eyebrows sardonically. 'I wish I'd caught on as quickly as you. I thought that perhaps Magda saw something in Tyler that I didn't.' He gave a short, dry laugh. 'Which she obviously did. But what she told me was that she thought that if we took Tyler in she'd be able to control him. She said she'd prove it the next time we visited my parents, which happened to be the following Christmas. Darned if he wasn't all sweetness and light while we were there, too. I was impressed, and hopeful, so, fool that I was, I suggested that we take Tyler back to New York with us. I wasn't so completely crazy that I offered to become his guardian right away. I said we'd try it for a while. But, back in New York, Tyler continued to be as good as gold. He hung around the apartment all of the time he wasn't in school, and stayed home nights, with no apparent desire to go out and get into mischief. I was so pleased that something had finally succeeded with Tyler that six months later I became his legal guardian. He was fifteen then.

'It wasn't long after that that Magda announced that she was pregnant. We hadn't been trying for a child, because she'd maintained that she wasn't ready. Now, she said that she'd forgotten her birth-control pills. She seemed happy about it, and I was delighted. Everything went along reasonably well for the next few months, in spite of the fact that Magda had to be very careful. No drinking, no sex, a lot of rest, the doctor told her. She seemed rather anxious and jittery, but I put it down to the fact that she was being denied two of her favourite pastimes. Then, one Saturday morning, I came home unannounced a day early from a trip. I was surprised when no one answered the door, but later found out that the staff had all been given the day off. When I let myself in, I heard strange moanings and groanings coming from the living-room. I went to look. Lying on a big fur rug, which Magda had recently bought, were she and Tyler, stark naked.' Lincoln stopped, his face contorted with disgust. 'Would you believe it?' he asked harshly.

Cassie could only shake her head, then contradict herself by saying weakly, 'I'm afraid, as far as Tyler is concerned, that I can.'

Lincoln nodded and sighed heavily. 'I realised then that it must have been going on for some time, but it still didn't occur to me that the child Magda was carrying wasn't mine.' He smiled wryly. 'I'm pretty naïve, or used to be. Anyway, Tyler got up and ran off as fast as he could to his room. I would have gone after him, except that after a couple of steps I looked back because of some kind of horrible moan that Magda let out. She was trying to stand up, but kept getting up part-way and then falling back down. I told her to snap out of it, she'd obviously had plenty of energy a few minutes before. She did manage to get to her feet then, but she kept weaving around, babbling incoherently. It was then that I noticed some blood on the rug. Very shortly, there was a great deal of blood. I called the ambulance and tried to get her in a position where the bleeding would stop, but it was no use. She was unconscious and haemorrhaging badly. She was, as they so bluntly put it on the death certificate, dead on arrival at the hospital. They, of course, took the baby immediately, but didn't think she'd live. I stayed there, night and day, praying for the tiny creature, watching her as if both our lives depended on it, still never imagining that she was anything but my own little girl.

'It was several months later, when I had Colleen home, that it suddenly hit me. I was congratulating myself on pulling her through, looking at the medical information on how many days old she was when the pregnancy was terminated. It didn't quite jib with how far along Magda had told me she was. I counted back to when it had begun. I was in Europe then, for almost a month. The baby was obviously Tyler's.' Lincoln closed his eyes and bowed his head. 'Heaven forgive me,' he whispered, 'but I've never felt quite the same about Colleen since. I know it's not sensible, I know it's wrong, but I can't seem to change the way I feel, especially when she misbehaves. Another Tyler, I think, and all I want to do is get away.' He raised his head and looked at Cassie, his jaw set. 'I will get over it, damn it! That was one of the decisions I made last night. Will you help me?'

Cassie blinked rapidly to clear away her tears. She had listened to Lincoln's sad story with an ache in her heart so strong that she almost feared it was a physical pain. How could anyone do such a thing to kind, gentle Lincoln? Had neither Tyler nor Magda cared that their moments of pleasure would cause him such agony? She put her hand over Lincoln's.

'Of course I'll help, all that I can,' she replied. 'I don't think you need to worry about Colleen's being another Tyler. I'm sure that once you alter your approach you'll see a change very quickly, although you'll have to expect her to keep testing you, just like any normal child. You'll have to be the one to initiate the changes, though, and spend enough time with Colleen to make them stick. I can't do that for you, but I'll back you up all the way, and I know that Mrs Lindstrom will, too.' She paused. 'I almost hate to ask this,' she said, 'but does Tyler know?'

Lincoln shook his head. 'As far as I know, he doesn't, although that's no guarantee. I certainly don't plan to tell him, ever. I do know he's never shown any interest in Colleen. He does go for redheads, though. He even had the gall to claim once that he loved Magda, and that's the reason he always seems to wind up with another redhead. I should have thought of that and warned you, but it never occurred to me that he'd try to attack you right in the house. But then, why should that have surprised me?'

'Maybe he did love Magda, in his own strange way,' Cassie said slowly. 'She gave him what he wanted most, and apparently made him behave the rest of the time to get it.' She thought of Willton's oblique reference to Magda's discontent. Had he known all along and said nothing? 'How did they manage to fool Willton?' she asked. 'I'm surprised that he didn't know what was going on and tell you about it. He doesn't miss very much.'

'Oh, he knew,' Lincoln said. 'He told me later, with tears in his eyes, that he just didn't know how to tell me.' He made a wry face. 'That's enough of the sordid story of my past for now. I've probably already convinced you that you don't want anything to do with such a gullible, inept fool.' He held Cassie's hand tightly, his eyes searching her face anxiously as if he thought she really might have decided that she wanted nothing more to do with him.

'Don't be ridiculous!' Cassie shook her head, then threw her arms around Lincoln's neck and pressed her cheek against his, her heart still aching at all he had endured, his scar-roughened cheek reminding her that there had been even more tragedy in his recent life. 'Being so kind and trusting that you don't see it when others aren't that way is not being a fool. I'd say it was a rare and beautiful gift, although it does make it doubly hard when people let you down so terribly.' She kissed her way across his cheek to his ear, then pulled her head back and smiled at him.

'I'm glad you haven't turned hard and cynical because of it. That would be a real tragedy, as far as I'm concerned. All of these years, whenever I've thought of you, the words "kind" and "loving" have been a part of your image.'

'Don't try to make a saint out of me,' Lincoln said gruffly. 'I'm capable of intense anger, as you've already seen, and I'm not nearly as trusting as I once was.' His arms tightened around Cassie. 'Until I met you again, I didn't think I'd ever trust another woman, but the way you say whatever is going on in your mind or your heart, and the way I myself can almost feel the way you're feeling, made me change my own mind about that overnight. Now, if I can just get my head straight about Colleen . . .'

'Your head is straight. I think you've gone through a perfectly dreadful experience and are still having trouble dealing with it, but who wouldn't? Especially with your recent . . . accident on top of it. Don't be so hard on yourself. Take one day at a time.' Cassie laughed softly. 'I give such good advice. Why don't I ever take it? My mother used to tell me that I was the worst trouble-borrower she'd ever seen. I can always get myself tied up in knots over dozens of things that might go wrong in the future, but probably won't.'

'Knowing what you should do and doing it are sometimes two very different things, aren't they?' Lincoln asked, looking into Cassie's eyes, the tension of a short time ago now gone from his face, replaced by the gentle, warm smile that Cassie loved to see. 'I hope I'm not giving you a lot of extra things to worry about.'

She smiled at him. 'When you smile at me like that, I can't think of a single thing,' she said. 'Everything is perfect.'

Lincoln's arms tightened around Cassie again. 'Ah, my little love,' he said, 'I feel the same way when you're in my arms. If only we could stay this way forever, like lovers in statue form, locked together for all eternity.'

'That sounds nice,' Cassie murmured. Then the image of the two of them as a statue flashed into her mind and a silly thought made her giggle. 'I'm not sure I'd like the snow in the winter though. And then, there'd be the birds...'

'Birds?' Lincoln asked, for a moment baffled. 'Oh, lord, Cassie!' He burst into uproarious laughter. 'I get the picture.' He sat back and grinned at Cassie. 'Well, now that the spell is broken, what do you say we go and find Colleen and see what I might get for her that would be both entertaining and useful in my new campaign. I don't even know how far she's gotten in learning her letters and numbers. I'd like her to get used to the idea of enjoying learning new things and being rewarded for doing so. That's always been one of Tyler's biggest problems. He has a good mind, but only uses it on rare occasions.'

'That's a great idea,' Cassie agreed. 'I'll bet you'll be surprised at how much she knows.' She paused as Lincoln got slowly to his feet and tucked his crutches under his arms. They started walking back towards the house. 'What happened to Tyler after... after Magda died? You said he'd been well-behaved while she was alive. Did he do well in school then, too?'

'He did reasonably well in school, though not as well as I thought he could. After she died, his grades dropped off even more. He was like a zombie for quite a while. I guess maybe you're right, he did love her after his fashion. And he was probably afraid of what I might do, even though I told him I didn't blame him any more than I did Magda for what happened, and that he'd have to answer to his conscience. I didn't think much about him, to tell the truth. Not enough, I guess. I was too wrapped up in my own problems. Then, within a few months, Tyler was back to being his former self. Truant from school, staying out after hours, stealing from me when I wouldn't give him money, and anything else you might name that was undesirable. I tried to discipline him, but nothing seemed to work. I've always wondered what would have happened if Magda had lived. I would have found out what was going on eventually.'

'You loved Magda a great deal, didn't you?' Cassie said softly. 'Even though when you were telling me about her, all you said was that you were attracted to her.'

'I loved an illusion,' Lincoln said bitterly. 'Let's not talk about it any more.'

'All right,' Cassie said quickly. 'Instead, let's talk about when we might take Colleen to visit my parents' farm. I've told both them and Colleen that we'd do that soon.'

Her diversion worked, erasing the lines of pain from Lincoln's face fairly fast. But later, as she watched him playing with Colleen, she more than once caught a fleeting look of deep sadness cross his face, even though he was warm and affectionate with the little girl. Perhaps, she thought, the fact that Colleen reminded him of Magda was really to blame for Lincoln's previous failure to spend time with her.

Colleen's occasional misbehaviour was too typically childlike to remind anyone of Tyler's deviations, nor was there anything about Colleen's appearance to remind him of the dark-haired, weasel-featured Tyler.

Maybe, Cassie thought, now that Lincoln had decided to spend a lot more time with Colleen, he would begin to recover from that terrible deception and be able to face the fact that he had lost someone he loved. She doubted he had ever done so, instead walling off his feelings for Magda in the time before that sad morning as if they didn't even exist. Another thought disturbed Cassie greatly. What if Cassie Lewis, with her red hair, was not the beginning of it all, but rather only a stepping-stone on Lincoln's way to facing the past, a temporary surrogate who let him get out feelings that he had too long kept hidden, even from himself?

'There I go, borrowing trouble again,' Cassie muttered to herself.

'What did you say?' Lincoln asked, looking over at her.

'I said that I've got to call Oggie Warren again,' Cassie invented quickly. 'I could start working with him next week if he's ready for me. I did tell you I'm going to be working for him part time when you were well enough, didn't I?' she added, as Lincoln looked perplexed.

Lincoln nodded. 'But I didn't realise it was so soon. It's just as well, though, because I've got to start attacking some of my piled-up mail. Willton says there's no more room on my desk.'

'Can I help?' Colleen asked, leaning against Lincoln's chair and staring at him hopefully with her big, green eyes.

Cassie could see Lincoln start to say no, then catch himself and laugh. 'I think I can use you part time,' he said. 'I wouldn't want a good helper like you just standing around with nothing to do. I'll find you a job.'

'Oh, boy!' Colleen said happily.

Later, when Colleen had gone, with a minimum of complaint, to take her nap, Lincoln closed the door to the nursery behind them and then asked, 'Well, how did I do? Any improvement?'

'About a hundred and fifty per cent,' Cassie replied. 'Think you can keep it up? It's not something you can do just once in a while, you know.'

'Yes, I know,' Lincoln said with a wry smile. 'I also know that being married to you will be something like spending my life with a small bulldog attached to one ankle. Once you get on to something, you don't let go.'

'Only if it's important,' Cassie said, making a face at him. 'But if you think you'll find my persistence unbearable, speak up. I'm not going to change, and I'd just as soon know if I'm about to be dropped from your list.'

'Not a chance,' Lincoln replied. 'Didn't you notice that I said I *will* be married to you?'

'I noticed. Aren't you getting a little ahead of yourself? I don't recall saying that I'd marry you yet.'

'You will. I'm more sure of it every moment we're together. Besides, you may be surprised to know that your mild-mannered Lincoln is famous in some circles for *his* persistence.'

'Are you sure you don't mean stubbornness?' Cassie teased. 'I'd certainly believe that.'

'I've been accused of that, too,' Lincoln said with a grin. He stopped and looked down the staircase. 'Here, take my crutches, will you? I think I'll go down without them using the railing.' He gave Cassie a defiant look as she took the crutches, frowning at him as she did so.

'I'm not saying anything,' she said, 'I'll just stand here and pray.' She assumed a prayerful pose, looking skywards.

'O ye of little faith,' Lincoln scolded, and then proceeded to negotiate the stairs carefully and successfully, one at a time, to the bottom.

From that day onwards, Cassie felt as if, in many ways, she was being treated to a sample of what marriage to Lincoln would be like. They shared mealtimes, time with Colleen in the mornings, and Cassie knew Lincoln would have been only too happy to share his bed with her if she would let him. He did not press the issue, but the ragged passion that sometimes overtook both of them when they kissed goodnight made it very clear that the idea was not far from either of their minds.

In the afternoons, Cassie went to Midvale College to work with Ogden Warren on preparations for the Shakespeare Festival. She found the problem of keeping Ogden organised so that none of the details of costumes, sets or lighting got behind schedule almost as exciting as being on stage.

'Thank the lord you're here, Cassie,' Ogden said more than once. 'You're quickly making yourself irreplaceable.'

'Exactly what I planned to do,' she told him, although her increasing involvement with the Festival added to her conflict over how she would eventually respond to Lincoln's determination to marry her. She felt increasingly sure of her love for him, but was still not convinced that she was not a replacement for Magda, rather than the other way around. What if some morning Lincoln awoke to the realisation that she was only a pale imitation of the beautiful, exciting woman whom he had loved and so cruelly lost?

She would brood about that at night, but in the morning Lincoln would be so openly warm and affectionate that she would wonder why she had worried. He seemed as delighted as Colleen with their visits to the Lewises' farm. Colleen was in wide-eyed heaven at the new sights and sounds of the farm, turning Cassie's parents into instant grandparents with her sunny smile and bright curls.

On their first visit, only two days after Lincoln had his cast removed, Cassie took advantage of the extra company to spirit off a load of clothing without having to answer questions about her reasons for staying on at Oak Hill. Her father tried. Just before Cassie got in her car to leave, he took her aside and asked, 'How much longer are you planning to stay over there? It doesn't look to me as if you're needed any more.'

'For a while,' Cassie answered vaguely, giving him a bright smile.

Just behind her father she heard her mother mutter in his ear, 'Oh, for goodness' sake, Henry! Sometimes I think you're the most unobservant man on earth.' Over his shoulder, she gave Cassie a little wink. 'Come again, real soon,' she said. 'All of you.'

'We will,' Cassie replied, wondering as she had all of her life if her mother really could see everything that was going on inside her just by looking into her eyes.

Even more pleasant, Cassie thought, than the activities she and Lincoln shared, were the quiet times when they sat together in the comfortably cluttered atmosphere of the small library at Oak Hill, which Lincoln had converted to a temporary office. With its book-filled walls, deep-cushioned chairs and a bay window overlooking a small garden, it was her favourite room at Oak Hill. In that pleasant room they shared stories of the past years when they had been apart.

Lincoln told Cassie of his life as an executive of a huge Wall Street brokerage firm. She not only learned a great deal about a subject which had hitherto been a mystery to her, but also sensed the truth of Willton's observation that Lincoln was not especially in love with his work, which he described as a 'rat race'.

'Do you plan to go back as soon as you've had your scars removed?' she asked, wishing that he would say no and at least one of her worries would be ended.

But Lincoln only shrugged. 'I'm not sure,' he said. 'I could stay here and take over the farms, but I haven't decided yet if that would satisfy me completely, either. I'm still going over various options.'

For her part, Cassie described graphically some of the traumas she had witnessed during her nurse's training, which led to her deep conflict over nursing as a career, and a feeling of guilt at not staying with it to help those in need.

'I think you cared too much,' Lincoln said gently, when only thinking of some of the tragedies again brought tears to Cassie's eyes. 'That's certainly not a fault.'

'That's what Kevin told me,' Cassie replied. 'He said there was no way I could keep trying to hold it all inside. I'd be like a doomsday clock, inching closer to zero every day.'

'Kevin?' Lincoln asked, and Cassie at last gathered her courage and told him of her two brief but intense romances with the Mayfield brothers which, she said, had left her wiser but not sadder, for she still liked both of them very much.

'They both sound like intelligent, interesting men,' Lincoln commented. 'I think I'm lucky you got cold feet both times. I guess I'd better hope you don't decide to cut and run from me one of these days.'

'It wasn't cold feet,' Cassie corrected him. 'It was a perfectly logical decision both times. There were a couple of things that really bothered me, and I didn't think they'd change. In fact, I knew they wouldn't. With Kevin it was his ungodly workload. With Martin, it was his travelling, and the women that followed him around. I wouldn't have trusted a saint with the temptations he's got constantly around him.'

'Then you're still evaluating me, calmly and logically?' Lincoln asked with an amused smile. He was sitting at his desk, his feet up, wearing old jeans and a sweatshirt, his hair still untouched by a barber's shears. Between his fingers was one of the cigars which he occasionally smoked.

'Certainly,' Cassie replied. 'I have a little checklist that I go over every night. Those cigars aren't getting you any gold stars, either.'

Lincoln grinned and took a puff on his cigar. 'If that's enough to scare you off, I don't want you,' he said. Then he suddenly pulled his feet to the floor and turned to face Cassie, his face serious. 'But I think I do know one thing that you're still worried about. Tyler.'

Cassie flinched visibly at the sound of that name. It was the first time in several weeks that Tyler had been mentioned, although Cassie had been brooding about him off and on, wondering whether she should bring the subject up. Even if all of her other questions were answered satisfactorily, she could never live in a home where that disgusting creature was welcome to come and go.

'He's definitely a sticking point,' Cassie admitted. 'I don't like to deliver ultimatums, but there's no way I could tolerate having him around. At all. Period.'

'I know,' Lincoln said, his expression grim. 'I plan to deal with that before very long. Tyler will not be bothering us after we're married.' He raised one questioning eyebrow at Cassie and took another puff of his cigar. 'What else is there?'

'I wish you wouldn't say "after we're married",' Cassie said, frowning as Lincoln smiled and said softly,

'But we will be.'

'Don't take me for granted,' she said sharply. 'I'm having the time of my life working on the Shakespeare Festival. If I left here it would mean passing up the most interesting job I'm apt to come across with my background and training. *If* I decided to marry you, and you plan to go back to New York, I'd have to give all that up, or else have one of those commuter marriages, which I wouldn't like at all.'

Lincoln scratched his head. 'Yes, that is a problem, isn't it?' He shrugged dismissively. 'We'll work it out. I wouldn't keep it on my list of major concerns if I were you. How are things going for the Festival? What stage are you at now?'

'Everything's coming together,' Cassie replied, feeling annoyed that Lincoln seemed to think her concern about her future career was of so little importance. 'You know, my career is just as important to me as yours is to you. It would help if you'd let me in on what you're planning to do.'

'Yes, my dear little bulldog, I do know,' Lincoln said impatiently. 'When I can tell you something, I will.'

'I don't see why it has to be such a mystery,' Cassie grumbled.

'Just take my word for it that it does,' Lincoln replied. 'Some time, but not now, I will explain exactly why. Now, how about the Festival? Is all I get a vague answer on that?'

'That's all you deserve,' Cassie said with a frown. 'Scenery is being built and painted, costumes made and fitted. We're rehearsing bits and pieces, since not all the actors will be here until next week, on June the first. Oggie's throwing a party for everyone then, and you're invited. I hope you'll come. I'd like you to meet the people I'm working with.'

'Think I look human enough?' Lincoln asked, running his hand across his face and frowning.

'Of course you do,' Cassie replied quickly. 'Your smaller scars don't show much any more. Unless you plan to have the others worked on before you show your face in public, you might as well start going out more. You aren't going to scare anyone.'

'I'm not sure when I'll get around to that surgery,' Lincoln said thoughtfully. 'At the moment, it's not high on my list of priorities. All right, I'll come along. I'm anxious to see the bearded Oggie Warren. Last time I saw him, he was trying to grow a moustache and could only manage a few straggly wisps.'

'Are you sure I won't scare anyone?' Lincoln asked the following week, after he had dressed for the party in the casual wear that Cassie had suggested, knowing that the party was mostly a chance for the working crew and actors to relax for one last time before the real rehearsals began. 'I thought maybe I'd try out for *Phantom of the Opera*.'

'You'd have a better shot at the Scarecrow in *The Wizard of Oz*,' Cassie replied, with a pointed lift of her eyebrows at Lincoln's hair.

'I like it this way,' Lincoln said, the defiant expression on his face reminding Cassie of Colleen at her worst. 'Back when the other kids had long hair, I always had to keep mine short because my parents equated long hair with sin. I've spent ten years on Wall Street in three-piece suits and the latest blow-dried hairstyles. Enough.'

'Lord 'a mercy, I've got a teenage rebel on my hands,' Cassie groaned. 'Would you like to wear an earring, too?'

'Will Mommy let me?' Lincoln teased.

'Sure,' she replied. 'I'll even pierce your ear for you.'

'No, thanks,' Lincoln said with an exaggerated shudder. 'I've been pierced enough lately.'

Now that Lincoln's leg was fully recovered, he drove them to the party in his car, a pleasantly comfortable old Cadillac. It had been left in storage in the carriage house at Oak Hill, and Max, whose mechanical talents were as remarkable as his way with plants, had helped Lincoln restore it to smooth running order.

'I can see why they don't make cars this size much any more,' Lincoln commented, as he tried to find a parking space near Ogden Warren's house on the edge of the campus of Midvale College. At last they found a space, parked, and walked to the brightly lit little house, where the sounds of a party already getting in full swing could be heard from several houses away.

'Theatre people are notoriously noisy. They all talk as if they have to project to the last row,' Cassie said, when Lincoln asked if the neighbours would complain before the night was over. 'I expect the neighbours have gotten used to Oggie by now.' She paused at the open door and peeped in to survey the crowd. There were so many people milling about that she could not see their host. 'Might as well go on in,' she said, looking up at Lincoln. 'We'll find Oggie . . .' She stopped. Carrying clearly over the buzz of other voices came tones so deep and beautifully mellow that she would have recognised them anywhere.

'Where's Cassandra?' asked the voice of Martin Mayfield. 'She's the one I came to see.'

Oh, joy, Cassie thought grimly. Lincoln was now going to be treated to the sight of Martin greeting her with his usual effusive passion, not knowing that Martin greeted every female the same way.

'That,' Cassie said, giving Lincoln a desperate look, 'is Martin Mayfield. I didn't know he was going to be here. Come on, I might as well get this over with. Please don't mistake his intentions towards me. He hugs and kisses all women a lot.' She took Lincoln's hand and led him forward, at the same time calling out, 'Martin! What in the world are you doing here?'

CHAPTER EIGHT

'CASSIE, my love!' boomed Martin's voice.

The way between them separated, as Lincoln observed later, like Moses' parting the Red Sea. Martin Mayfield was not an extremely handsome man, but the charisma which projected itself past the footlights made him seem more handsome than he was, somehow larger than life. He came towards Cassie, his arms outstretched. 'I've come to see the woman who still owns my heart,' he said.

At the sound of those words, Lincoln let go of Cassie's hand and put his arm possessively around her shoulders.

'How sweet of you, Martin,' Cassie said, watching Martin cast a quick, appraising glance at Lincoln and then quickly lower his arms so that he could take the hand that Cassie held out to him, 'but I know that I'm just one of many stockholders.'

Martin's eyes sparkled with that peculiar intensity that Cassie still found attractive. 'Still as sharp and untamed as ever, I see,' Martin said, carrying Cassie's hand to his lips and kissing it lingeringly. Then he looked up at Lincoln, who was several inches taller. 'Your latest Petruchio?' he asked, raising his beautifully arched brows.

'Not exactly, Martin,' Cassie replied, feeling annoyed with both Martin and with Lincoln, whose grip on her shoulders felt more like a wrestler's hold. 'This is Lincoln Snow, an old friend of mine, who needed my services as a nurse after a nearly fatal accident.'

'Oh, yes. Ogden mentioned something about that,' Martin said. He shook Lincoln's hand. 'Glad to see you've survived so well. And now you've succumbed to Cassandra's nearly fatal charms.'

'Nice to see that you've recovered from that affliction,' Lincoln replied, his voice loaded with sarcasm.

'Stop it or I won't have anything to do with either of you,' Cassie snapped, glaring at first Martin and then Lincoln. She spotted Ogden Warren, standing a little off to the side and watching the exchange between Martin and Lincoln with interest. 'Oggie,' she purred, 'why didn't you tell me that Martin was going to be here tonight?' She hadn't mentioned the romantic involvement between herself and Lincoln to him, so she knew that he could not have deliberately planned to create a difficult situation, but he did not need to look as if he was enjoying it so much.

'I didn't know until late this afternoon myself or I would have,' Ogden said quickly, obviously catching the gleam in Cassie's eyes that threatened fireworks. He came forward, smiling, his hand held out to Lincoln. 'Link, old friend,' he said, 'I can't tell you how happy I am to see you looking so hale and hearty. Can we in Midvale dare to hope that you'll be back among us for good?'

'You're certainly free to hope,' Lincoln replied, looking amused at Ogden's stilted speech. 'I'm impressed with that beard, Oggie. Is it really yours?'

Ogden looked startled, then laughed, most of the pseudo-British accent disappearing as he replied. 'It's all mine. You're remembering when I tried to grow a moustache, aren't you? The summer when we were both madly in love with Felicia Arbuckle.'

'Lord, that's right,' Lincoln said, shaking his head. 'I'd forgotten all about Felicia. I wonder what became of her?'

'I don't know,' Ogden replied. 'I only remember her because it was the summer after we did *Romeo and Juliet* in Miss Pilchard's drama class, and she was Juliet to my Romeo. That was the start of all of this.' Ogden waved his arm towards the rest of the room. 'I found my niche in life early.' He eyed Lincoln curiously. 'Are you really a big-time wheeler-dealer in Wall Street? Somehow, I always thought of you as more the poetic type, in spite of your athletic prowess. I always expected that you'd turn out to be a writer of some kind.'

Watching Lincoln's face as Ogden talked, Cassie saw him suddenly look at Ogden with a new intensity and respect.

'Did you? It's only been in recent years that I thought I might have missed my calling,' Lincoln said. 'I went straight from college to Wall Street without thinking of anything else.'

Ogden nodded sagely. 'Family expectations,' he said. 'My father thought I was crazy when I wanted to go into the theatre instead of taking over the hardware store. Say...' he took hold of Lincoln's arm '...let's get a drink and talk about old times.' He jerked his thumb towards Cassie. 'Cassie can take care of herself.'

Lincoln looked down at Cassie, then at Martin Mayfield. 'I expect she can,' he replied, giving her shoulders a little hug before following Ogden towards the bar set up at the far end of the room.

Cassie was not sure whether to sigh with relief or scream with frustration, for as soon as Lincoln had moved off Martin took hold of her arm and moved closer. 'I think maybe we ought to talk over old times, too,' he said in her ear. 'I hope you're not getting serious about that Snow fellow. I haven't given up my quest yet, either.'

'Please let go, Martin,' Cassie said in a low voice. 'I am not in the mood to be treated like a steak caught between two hungry wolves. Yes, I am serious about Lincoln and I would just as soon you didn't make life difficult for me by clutching at me and breathing down my neck like that.'

'Oh, the jealous type, is he?' Martin scoffed, ignoring her request. 'I can see why he'd need to be.'

'The fact that he's scarred right now has nothing to do with anything,' Cassie growled, so angry that she could scarcely keep from slapping Martin's face. 'There are other factors that I'm not even slightly interested in explaining to you. Now, if you don't mind, I think I'll get myself a drink.'

'I'm sorry,' Martin said, looking instantly contrite. 'Let me get us both a drink and then we'll have our own cosy little talk. I wanted to tell you what I've been doing this past year. I've got greetings from Kevin, and also some other news that I think you'd be very interested to hear.'

'All right,' Cassie agreed. 'Soda and lime for me.'

'How could I forget?' Martin teased with a warmly seductive smile. 'I doubt your Mr Snow wants to carry you home over his shoulder like a sack of rags. I'll be right back. Don't go away.'

As if I could, Cassie thought grimly. The living-room of Ogden's house was rapidly becoming packed, the sound-level making it difficult to hear anyone more than a foot away. She looked towards the bar, but could not see Lincoln's familiar brown mop anywhere. He and Ogden had probably decided to find a quieter spot. She pushed her way towards the bar, hoping to find it a little less crowded at that end of the room, but met Martin coming her way, their drinks raised over his head and a dramatic frown ridging his forehead.

'Oggie had better get a bigger house or have smaller parties,' he shouted at Cassie. 'Let's try the back yard. There's a patio out there.'

Cassie nodded and followed him.

'Phew,' Martin said, once they were outside. 'I don't mind a crush, but that's too much. Hot, too.' He handed Cassie her drink and raised his towards her. 'To us,' he said, 'and what might have been a beautiful life together. Still could be, if you'd listen to reason.'

'I'm not good at that,' Cassie replied with a smile. 'Now, what's all this news you have from Kevin and elsewhere?'

'Kevin wanted me to tell you that he's decided to specialise in endocrinology. It's my guess that he may even decide to become a researcher instead of a practitioner. At any rate, he sends his love and wants to stay on your short-list, too.'

'Tell him that I appreciate the thought,' Cassie said with a sigh. 'I'll be happy for him if he does that. I think he's more inclined that way. He hated emergency work almost as much as I did.'

'I know,' Martin said, leaning comfortably against a maple tree and taking a long draught of his drink. 'The other news is that, although this past year was pretty much run of the mill for the company, next year's definitely going to be something special. We've got bookings into several major theatres, including the Kennedy Center next April for a special series in celebration of Shakespeare's birthday.'

'That's wonderful,' Cassie said enthusiastically. 'I can't say that I'm surprised, though. You deserve it.'

'Thank you,' Martin said with a gracious nod. 'How would you like to be a part of it?'

'M-me?' Cassie stammered. She could hear the ice in her glass tinkle, as her hand started to shake, and her heart started to pound. The implications of Martin's suggestion were only an amorphous cloud in her head, but she knew without thinking that they were tremendous.

'You,' Martin replied, smiling and leaning towards her. 'We're expanding the company, and we're going to need a first understudy for several of the major roles. You know as well as I do that if you took the job, you'd have several opportunities to perform. No season goes by without some kind of trauma or illness putting the lead out of commission for a while.'

'I-I'd have to think about it,' Cassie said, her head spinning with visions of the beautiful costumes and superb performers of the really top-flight Shakespearian company with which Martin worked. 'I was very seriously thinking of taking the job here at Midvale College that Ogden offered me.'

'Ah, but that's nothing like being really in the thick of it, is it?' Martin said softly, his hand caressing Cassie's cheek. 'Imagine playing Ophelia to my Hamlet.' He leaned closer and touched his lips to Cassie's. 'Or Juliet to my Romeo,' he whispered. His arms suddenly went behind Cassie's neck and he pressed his lips against hers. 'Oh, Cassie,' he said in anguished tones, 'how can you have forgotten the passion we shared? Can't you give us another chance?'

The sound of a door slamming brought Cassie back to reality as suddenly as a splash of ice-cold water. What if Lincoln had seen her just now? 'Stop it, Martin,' she said, pushing him away and turning, trying vainly to see who or what had caused the noise. There was no one in sight. 'I hope that wasn't Lincoln,' she muttered. She turned and frowned at Martin Mayfield. 'For a moment there, I'd forgotten that you're a marvellous actor. "How can you have forgotten the passion we shared?"' she mimicked, his own anguished tones exaggerated. 'How many women have you used that one on?'

Martin shrugged. 'It does seem to work rather well,' he said. 'But I am seriously offering you the job. I hope you'll think it over. It could be a really big step up for you.'

'I know,' Cassie said. She studied Martin. That special, magical aura that had so entranced her before had faded, rather quickly this time, disappearing in the realisation that he could, and frequently did, act just as well off the stage as on. There was nothing between them like the deep, profound magic between her and Lincoln. Was there enough magic in a career on the stage to replace that? Could glitter and make-believe ever replace the warm, loving glow of Lincoln's smile? Deep inside, Cassie felt something click into place, like a gear suddenly meshing with its mate. The answer was so clear. Nothing in the world could bring her the joy that sharing her life with Lincoln would bring. Not in a million years!

Cassie smiled and shook her head firmly. 'I'm afraid not, Martin,' she said. 'Unless something changes dramatically here, I think I'd rather stay in Midvale.'

'Even if your Lincoln Snow doesn't?' Martin asked. 'Or haven't things gone that far yet?'

'No comment,' Cassie replied. Martin Mayfield was not going to be the first to know what she had just decided! 'Now, if you'll excuse me, I think I'd better find Lincoln.' She felt a strong urge to get away from this crowd and tell Lincoln of her decision as soon as possible. The thought of how his eyes would glow with happiness when she told him that she loved him and would marry him made her heart start beating faster.

'I'll go for another drink myself,' Martin said, sighing heavily. 'I'm disappointed in you, Cassie. But, if you come to your senses in the next few weeks, let me know. I'm not ready to give up hope.'

'Suit yourself,' Cassie replied. She opened the door and slipped inside, surveying the room. As soon as she saw Lincoln, the joy in her heart evaporated. He was standing near the door, alone, watching the crowd, his expression grim and withdrawn. Oh, lord, Cassie thought, he did see Martin kiss me. And he definitely did not look as if he would be receptive to any calm explanations. She pushed her way through the crowd to his side as quickly as she could, not even trying to think of what she would say to him. All that she could think of when she reached him was, 'Hi. Are you ready to go home?' She felt as if she would become physically ill at the bleak unhappiness she saw in his eyes when he looked at her.

'Any time,' was all that he said. Then he turned and went out of the door.

Lincoln was silent as they walked to his car, silent on the drive to Oak Hill, and silent as they went inside. Unable to decide what, if anything, to say, Cassie remained silent also, wishing that Lincoln would say just anything to break the frozen quiet. At the foot of the staircase he stopped, while Cassie started up, so miserable that she was at first unaware that he was not beside her.

'Cassie!' Lincoln's voice was harsh.

Cassie turned and looked at him. His face was no longer unhappy, it was totally, unforgivingly, cold and blank. 'W-what?' she stammered.

'I suggest that you pack your things. I expect you to be ready to leave in the morning,' he said. With that, he turned and walked rapidly towards his office, his head down.

Cassie's knees became wobbly and she sat down with a thud on the staircase, staring after Lincoln, unable and unwilling to believe what she had heard him say. 'He can't mean it,' she whispered, tears beginning to roll down her cheeks. 'He can't mean it. But he does!' Cassie tried to struggle to her feet, but felt too sick and dizzy to do so. She sat down again and buried her face in her hands, sobbing. Before it had even started, her life with Lincoln was over. And all because of that blasted Martin Mayfield! It was too awful to be true. She tried to stop crying, but each time a vision of Lincoln's cold, hard face came before her and she sobbed anew, shivering as if the coldness of his eyes had penetrated into her entire body. A few minutes later, the touch of a hand on her shoulder startled her so that she nearly lurched forward off the step where she sat.

'Miss Cassandra, what's wrong?' came Willton's voice, his face a watery blur through Cassie's tears.

'Everything,' she sobbed, shaking her head. 'Everything. I wish I were dead.' She sobbed harder than ever as Willton bent and peered into her face.

'You don't mean that, Miss Cassandra,' he said, pressing a pristine handkerchief into her shaking hand. When Cassie only held it, he took it back and grasped her arm firmly. 'Come with me,' he said, urging her to her feet. 'Come along, now. Carefully. Don't fall. That's right.'

'Can't come,' Cassie mumbled, stumbling along beside Willton. 'Got to pack.'

Willton ignored her, leading her into the dining-room, carefully pulling out a chair and seating her in it, and then placing the brandy decanter and a large snifter with a hefty shot of brandy in it in front of her. He put the handkerchief into her hands again and sat down beside her. 'Dry your eyes, Miss Cassandra,' he ordered, 'and then tell me what happened. I've already taken Mr Snow a bottle of his favourite Scotch, so I know something is amiss. I wouldn't presume to order Mr Snow to tell me what is wrong, but I think that you and I . . . are quite good friends. I feel that it's my duty to be of some assistance to you, if I can, after all that you've done for Mr Snow.' When Cassie only stared at the old man morosely, he frowned very slightly. 'Come, now, Miss Cassandra,' he said, 'it's not like you to give up so quickly. Did I hear you say something about packing?'

Cassie nodded, then mopped at her face and blew her nose. 'Lincoln told me to pack and get out,' she said. She picked up the brandy snifter and took a large swallow. '"I expect you to be ready to leave in the morning'' is what he said.' She took another large swallow.

'Not too quickly,' Willton said, retrieving the snifter from Cassie's grasp. 'Now, if you don't mind, tell me why Mr Snow made such a rash request. I find it difficult to believe that you've done something to deserve it.'

'He thinks I have,' Cassie said dully. 'Maybe I did.' She took the brandy glass back again. 'I'd rather be drunk,' she muttered, tilting her head back and taking another gulp. 'If I can't be dead, I'd rather be drunk.'

'Miss Cassandra!' Willton scolded. 'If you keep this up, I shall have to get you and Mr Snow together and knock your heads together. I'm too old to put up with this kind of nonsense from my two favourite people!'

'Your two favourite people?' Cassie smiled weakly at Willton. She was beginning to feel a little warmer now. There was almost a rosy glow about Willton's kindly face. 'Gosh, Willton, thank you,' she said. 'You're one of my favourite people, too.' When Willton only raised his eyebrows and pursed his mouth impatiently she made a face at him. 'OK, OK,' she said. 'I'll tell you what happened. Itsh...it's no wonder Lincoln's mad at me. I mean, if he saw that phoney Romeo Martin Mayfield kissing me he probably thinks I'm just another Magda. See, he's told me all about her and Tyler...' Cassie finished off the brandy with another gulp and then hiccuped. ''Scuse me. OK, the whole misherble story goes like this, Willton. I went out in the back yard with Martin...hey, you don't even know that I was almost engaged to him once, do you? Well, I was. Anyway...'

Cassie meandered through her story, pausing now and then to wipe away a fresh cascade of tears, concluding morosely, 'So you see, Willton, I've messed everything up. And right after I decided that I wanted to marry Lincoln, too. Now he's never going to want me.' She sniffled into the handkerchief and hiccuped again. 'I'm sorry,' she said. 'I guess I better go and start packing.'

Willton shook his head and sighed. 'I expect you ought to go to bed,' he said, 'but I don't like to see this go on any longer than necessary. I think you and Mr Snow had better have it out right now.'

'Oh, no!' Cassie said, her heart pounding at the thought of confronting Lincoln. 'I couldn't. Not now.' She stared at Willton, who almost bodily lifted her to her feet.

'Now,' he said firmly. 'You've done nothing to be ashamed of. Just explain things to Mr Snow as you have to me.' He grasped Cassie's arm again and began propelling her in the direction of Lincoln's office.

'He won't listen,' Cassie complained, weaving dizzily along at Willton's side. 'Beshides, I'm not in very good shape to...to 'splain anything.'

'You'll manage,' Willton said drily. He tapped on Lincoln's closed door, and then opened it without waiting for a reply. 'Miss Cassandra has something to tell you,' he said, ignoring Lincoln's glare and helping Cassie towards a chair near Lincoln's.

'Willton, have you lost your mind?' Lincoln growled. 'Take her away. I don't want to see her or hear her.'

'No, sir, I will not,' Willton replied calmly. 'There has been a misunderstanding, and I will not stand idly by this time and let things go from bad to worse.' He almost pushed the reluctant Cassie into her chair. 'I shall be waiting outside the door,' he said. 'I do not wish to hear any unreasonable shouting, nor the sounds of any objects breaking.' So saying, he turned stiffly and walked quietly out of the door, with Cassie and Lincoln staring after him in disbelief.

When the door had closed behind Willton, Lincoln swung his gaze towards Cassie, scowling darkly.

'I din't want to come,' she said hoarsely, shaking her head, her insides trembling strangely at the sight of Lincoln's anger. 'I really din't. But Willton told me I had to tell you what I told him and I hadda do it t'night.' When Lincoln's frown became more curious than hostile she added, 'I know I sound funny, but Willton made me drink a whole lot of brandy. I can't drink that stuff. It hits me just like a brick. I can't hardly stand up. Go ahead, laugh at me,' she added, seeing the corners of Lincoln's mouth twitch slightly. She sniffled and then blew her nose again in the damp handkerchief. 'I can't help it if I can't hold my liquor. But at least I'm not so stupid that I jump to stupid conclusions without even asking anyone whatsh going on.'

Lincoln raised one eyebrow at Cassie. 'I assume I'm the stupid person you're talking about?'

'You bet your boots you are,' she replied, frowning. 'Good old "God's gift to every woman" Mayfield convinced me that I ought 'ta marry you, and what do you do? You get some crazy ideas all wound up like a pretzel inside your head and tell me I've gotta get out. Maybe you just don't really love me after all. Maybe you just thought you did, because I remind you of Magda, not the other way around. Y'know, I was gonna ask you about that. I almost forgot. Now what's so funny?' she demanded, for Lincoln was now convulsed with silent laughter and wiping tears from his eyes with the back of his hands.

'You are,' Lincoln replied, shaking his head. He turned to face Cassie, then patted his knee and beckoned to her. 'Come over here,' he said.

Cassie stared at him. 'You aren't mad at me any more?'

'No. And I don't want you to doubt for another second that I love you and no one else. But I still want to hear what you told Willton,' Lincoln replied.

'Oh. OK.' Cassie put her hands on the arms of her chair and started to get up. The room tilted to the left and then veered to the right. 'I don't think I'm going any place,' Cassie said, sitting down again and clutching hard at the chair arms. 'This boat's in an awful storm.'

'I'll see if I can rescue you,' Lincoln said, moving to stand in front of Cassie. He bent forward. 'Can you manage to put your arms around my neck?'

'Oh, sure,' Cassie replied. She did so, and Lincoln immediately lifted her and carried her back to his chair.

'There,' he said, adjusting her limp body to sit on his lap, her head against his shoulder. 'No wonder you slept so well that night we had a little brandy and I rubbed your back. You can't drink at all, can you?'

'Uh-uh,' Cassie said, shaking her head. 'I learned that a long time ago. But I felt so awful . . .' Her eyes filled with tears again. 'How could you think I kissed Martin Mayfield?' she demanded, sitting up and staring into Lincoln's eyes accusingly. 'He kissed me, but I didn't kiss him back.'

'I couldn't tell that from where I stood,' Lincoln replied. 'I'd have had to have been standing only inches away to know that.'

'Well, that's where you should have been,' Cassie said, frowning. 'You should have heard him. Quote "Oh, if only we could recapture the passion we shared" unquote. I asked him how many women's he used that one on. He said it worked real well, so I expect it's a bunch. He was trying to talk me into going with his company as an understudy, so I guess he thought it was worth a try.'

'I see.' Lincoln traced the edge of Cassie's cheek, his eyes thoughtful as he looked into hers. 'I'm not sure I understand what happened. Did I hear you say something about deciding to marry me? I don't want you making decisions like that, just because Willton's been plying you with brandy.'

'Oh, no, no, no.' Cassie's hair swished back and forth as she shook her head vigorously. 'I decided that when I was thinking about Martin's offer at the party. All I had to drink there was soda and lime. I juss didn't think I'd like being on the stage as much as I'd like being your wife. I mean, glitter and stuff is neat, but you're... neater.' She giggled. 'Much neater. I 'specially like your hair that way. Did I ever tell you how much I like your hair that way?'

'Not recently,' Lincoln replied with a grin. He hugged Cassie close, his cheek against hers. 'My funny, adorable little angel,' he said, nuzzling her ear with his lips. 'If you still want to marry me in the morning, we'll see about getting you a ring. Right now, I think I'd better put you to bed.'

'In your bed?' Cassie asked. She pushed herself back and smiled brightly at Lincoln. 'I'd like that. I really would.' When Lincoln's face suddenly looked bleak she felt a cold chill run through her body. 'Brrr,' she said, blinking back a fresh batch of tears. 'What did I say wrong now? Don't you want me to sleep with you?'

Lincoln shook his head. 'I don't think this is a good time for a serious discussion. It's not important.'

'Oh, yes, it is,' Cassie contradicted. 'I can tell by your face. I told you everything, now you tell me. That's only fair.'

'All right,' Lincoln said with a sigh. 'As a matter of fact, I wasn't bothered nearly so much by seeing you kissing Martin Mayfield as I was by suddenly re-alising how extremely jealous it made me to see another man paying that kind of attention to you. I don't want to be jealous and unreasonable. I don't ever want you to be hurt because of something left over from my past. I want to conquer that before we make love and, to all intents and purposes, cut off your avenue of escape.' He reached for a Kleenex and dabbed at the tears that were running down Cassie's cheeks as she stared at him silently. 'You see, I was right. This is no time to analyse that problem.'

'I don't think there's a problem,' Cassie said slowly, caressing Lincoln's hair back from his forehead. 'It's perfectly understandable that you'd feel that way, after what Magda did, and it may take quite a while for you to get over it and know that you can always trust me. But you can, my love, and we don't need to wait. I want you to know right now that I'm yours, and only yours, forever.' She pressed her lips together tightly, her heart aching at the sadness she still saw in Lincoln's eyes. She flung her arms around his neck and clutched him tightly. 'Don't look so sad! I love you so much. I can't bear it that I hurt you,' she wailed.

'Oh, my darling, I'm not sad because of what you did,' Lincoln said hoarsely. 'I'm sad because I hurt you when I didn't need to. I sometimes forget how very sensitive and perceptive you are. Can you forgive me?'

'Of course I can. Can you forgive me?' Cassie said, trying hard to control her tears and hugging Lincoln's neck even tighter.

Lincoln coughed. 'I think I'll recover if you don't strangle me,' he said, reaching back to loosen Cassie's grasp. 'Come on, little angel, I think Willton's mission is accomplished. I'm taking you to bed, in my bed. I'll rub your back, and I doubt if I'll hear another peep out of you until morning. You'll be about as exciting to sleep with as a sack of flour.'

Cassie smiled. 'But I'll be fine in the morning,' she whispered in his ear.

CHAPTER NINE

SOMETHING tickled Cassie's cheek. She opened her eyes. 'How's your head this morning?' said a soft voice in her ear.

'My head?' For only a second, Cassie did not understand the question. Then, suddenly, she remembered. She was in Lincoln's bed, and that was Lincoln's voice behind her, and his arm around her! 'My head's fine,' she said, turning to face him, her arms sliding around to hold him fiercely against her for a moment. Then she released him and drew back, laying her hand along his cheek. 'Good morning,' she said, smiling into eyes that seemed to glow with their own captured sunlight. 'Have you been awake long?'

'Not very,' Lincoln replied, one hand exploring up and down Cassie's back beneath the short, camisole-like satin nightgown that she wore. 'But long enough for the thought of you lying there so close to me in that almost non-existent nightie to drive me wild.'

'How wild?' Cassie asked. 'Ooh,' she said after a quick exploration of her own. 'That wild.'

Lincoln chuckled. 'I almost wakened you in the middle of the night, but I wasn't sure you'd appreciate it after what that brandy did to you. I'm amazed you're not hung over.'

'I never have been,' Cassie replied. 'I guess the effects go as quickly as they come. You should have wakened me. I woke up once, too, and looked at you for the longest time in the moonlight. I touched you,

148

and when I discovered you weren't wearing any pyjamas I wanted so much to kiss you and wake you up, but I wasn't sure you'd appreciate it, either. You looked so perfectly relaxed and contented.'

'Don't ever let that stop you again,' Lincoln said with a smile. 'There are things I enjoy a lot more than being relaxed and contented.' He pulled Cassie close to him again and nestled his cheek against her hair. 'I want you so much,' he whispered, 'but I need to know if you're absolutely sure now. What about the Shakespeare Festival, and the job here?'

Cassie sighed. 'I'll have to stay with the Festival this summer, so I guess we ought to put off getting married until after it's over if you're going back to New York. If you are, I'll just have to see what I can find to do there.' She felt Lincoln's arms tighten around her and looked up at him. 'Have you decided yet?' she asked.

'I'm staying here,' he replied, laughing as Cassie let out a whoop of joy. 'I really don't want you to think that I was testing you in some way,' he went on when she had settled back into his arms with a sigh of relief. 'It's just that now that I know you're going to be my wife, you have a right to know some things that I won't tell anyone else for a little while yet. I've had my personal effects packed and they're being sent here, but I haven't put my apartment on the market, because I don't want to send a signal that I'm leaving permanently. It may amaze you to know that as I am a market analyst my opinion has carried an unreasonable amount of weight, so that I have to be very circumspect in the manner of my pulling out of the business. Otherwise, a lot of people will misinterpret my leaving as being either bullish or bearish for the market and possibly lose a lot of money.'

'I guess I didn't realise you were that important,' Cassie said, smoothing her hand up and down Lincoln's bare back. 'Do you mean that you're not going to do that at all any more?'

'I don't know. I'll see if after a while I have any desire to get back into it. For the present, I'm going to learn more about farm management and take over Oak Hill farms when I'm ready. At the same time, I plan to try some writing. Old Oggie hit the nail right on the head when he guessed it was something I'd be interested in doing. I've done a lot of straight expository writing already, of course, but I want to try my hand at fiction. Over the years, I've jotted down a lot of ideas.'

'Lincoln, my love, that sounds just wonderful,' Cassie said, kissing his neck. 'That means you'll be home a lot, just as my dad always was. I think that makes it a lot easier to raise a family.'

'I like that idea better, too,' Lincoln replied. 'Only seeing the kids when you're tired and tense after a hard day at the office isn't my idea of the way to go on. Sometimes I think Tyler might have turned out better if my dad had been here more of the time. He was too much for my mother to handle, with all of the other kids she had to keep an eye on. I don't know if I could have done anything with him, but I must admit I didn't try very hard after Magda died.'

'I don't think anyone would blame you for that,' Cassie said. 'Not that I want to keep talking about Tyler right now, but what do you plan to do to keep him away from us?'

Lincoln shifted Cassie so that he could look into her face. His expression was so serious and stern that she shuddered involuntarily and felt Lincoln's arms tighten around her. 'I won't have to do anything,' he said. 'The state will take care of that for me.'

'The state? Do you mean . . . prison?'

Lincoln nodded sadly. 'When Tyler left here, I gave him firm instructions to stay away and to stick to the straight and narrow until his twenty-first birthday, which is coming up in just three weeks. At that time, he'll come into a sizeable trust fund and I'll no longer be responsible for him in any way. Something told me he wouldn't do as I suggested, since he wanted far more money than I gave him, so I hired a couple of private investigators to check up on his activities. They've come up with enough evidence so that I can easily charge him with forgery and grand theft. I still hate to do that, since he's my sister's only son, but I'm not the only one who's been hurt by his activities. I can't withhold the evidence. Given his other brushes with the law, I doubt that he'll be put on probation. In fact, my lawyer tells me that he'll probably be in prison for several years. So, in a couple of weeks, I'll have to go back to New York for long enough to discharge my last duties as Tyler's guardian, give a deposition on his crimes, and say goodbye to Wall Street. I'm not looking forward to any of it.'

'I don't blame you,' Cassie said, gently brushing back the lock of hair that fell across Lincoln's forehead, 'but I must admit that I'll feel a lot better with Tyler behind bars. I still have nightmares where I see the look on his face when he attacked me that night. I think he's a dangerous man. I hope when he gets out of prison he isn't looking for revenge.'

'Let's cross that bridge when we come to it,' Lincoln said. He folded his arms around Cassie again and tucked her against him. 'Poor little angel. I didn't know you were having nightmares, too. I've been plagued with some myself.' He gave a short little laugh. 'Here we are, two of the luckiest people in the world and we still have our share of problems, but I guess that's nothing new. Wasn't it Shakespeare who said that the course of true love never runs smoothly?'

'Who else?' Cassie replied.

'Who indeed?' Lincoln said with a grin. 'According to Oggie, Shakespeare said everything that was worth saying for all time. However, I don't remember that he ever said, Cassie, let me take off your nightgown. I'm tired of having anything at all between us.'

Cassie laughed as she helped Lincoln slide her nightgown over her head. 'Maybe he wouldn't have thought that was worth saying,' she said.

Lincoln tossed Cassie's nightgown aside and then threw back their covers. 'Oh, yes, he would, my love,' Lincoln said, his voice husky with passion as he gazed at her and then stroked her body delicately, first caressing her breasts and slowly letting his hand find its way downwards. 'I think he would have looked for a hundred different ways to say it.'

'Mmm.' Cassie took a deep breath and let out a blissful sound of pleasure as Lincoln's lips followed the trail his fingers had blazed. She closed her eyes, letting the agonising pleasure of the waves of desire he created course through her and build, one upon another. When Lincoln took his attention away from a gentle tantalising of her rosy-peaked breasts to lean up on one elbow and drop little, soft kisses all over her forehead and cheeks, Cassie opened her eyes again to revel in the blurred image of the dear face that she adored, so close now, and finally truly hers. 'It's going to be so nice to have you around at home a lot,' she murmured, combing her fingers through his hair as he continued his shower of kisses, making a game of trying to catch him with kisses of her own while all the time the longing within her grew ever stronger. Her arms went around him, urging him to move over her.

Lincoln did so, propping himself on both arms so that he could look down at Cassie. 'I may never get any work done,' he said, his eyes dark and glowing with happiness. 'But I guess if I'm going to be a real farmer or a writer we'll have to use some discipline now and then. Which reminds me...' he reached under his pillow and produced a small packet '...we don't want to start any additions to the family until we're officially married.'

Cassie chuckled softly. 'Did Willton have a supply?'

'I forgot to ask,' Lincoln replied with a grin. He tucked his arms around Cassie again and slowly lowered his weight upon her, beginning to move his lips to hers and then opening his mouth wide to devour her eager response. Cassie groaned and clung to him, arching towards him, the world fading away in an increasingly wild concatenation of sensations. The roughness of Lincoln's chest, the hot, hard insistence of his own desire made her gasp with a sudden, urgent onslaught of sheer longing for fulfilment.

'I can't wait much longer,' she said hoarsely.

Wordlessly, Lincoln moved to take possession of her, at first slowly, then with such a fiery strength that Cassie gasped again and again at the beautiful madness of the passion unleashed within her, a madness that set the world spinning crazily and left two lovers rocketing through space on a ship that they alone could fly. Then, suddenly, the ship looped around the sun and gradually came back to orbit its home planet once again, settling slowly back to the earth from which it had sprung, landing as softly as a feather.

Cassie lay very still, her eyes closed, afraid to move and break what was surely a magical spell. When Lincoln at last stirred she opened her eyes, not at all surprised to see that his eyes were moist as he looked down at her, his lips smiling his warmest, most loving smile.

'I love you, Cassie,' he said. Then he crushed her tightly in his arms, his cheek against hers. 'Dear heaven, how much I love you,' he said again. 'How have I ever managed to live this long without you?'

'Or I without you?' she asked. She stroked his hair and breathed deeply. 'I guess maybe life had to get us ready for this,' she said. 'I'm sure I wasn't only a few years ago.'

'Maybe that's it,' Lincoln agreed. He kissed Cassie again and rolled to one side and sat up. 'Now that we've seen paradise,' he said with a smile, 'let's start making some plans for life on this dull old earth.' He got up and tossed Cassie her robe. 'How would the soon-to-be Mrs Snow like to take a shower with me and then discuss our future over breakfast?'

'Why, Mr Snow, what a romantic idea,' Cassie said with a delighted laugh.

A short time later, as they sat at the table in the morning room waiting for Willton to bring their breakfast, Cassie said, 'The first item on my agenda is to decide on a wedding date. The Festival runs from July the fifth through to the twenty-third. How about August the first?'

Lincoln nodded. 'I hate to wait that long, but that sounds reasonable. However, I don't want you to tell anyone until I'm back from New York.'

'Not even my parents?' Cassie asked. 'Why not?' as Lincoln shook his head.

'Superstitious, I guess,' Lincoln said with a grimace. 'I want to be sure everything is under control before we go public.'

'Under control? Are you talking about Tyler, or everything?'

'Mostly Tyler,' Lincoln admitted. 'It may seem unreasonable, but I won't really be able to enjoy myself making wedding plans or having parties until I have that session with Tyler and the law over with.'

Cassie bit her lip and studied Lincoln thoughtfully. When he talked about Tyler, he did look tense. 'You aren't going to be in any danger from him, are you?' she asked. 'He's bound to be furious.' In spite of Lincoln's denial, she still suspected that Tyler had had something to do with Lincoln's nearly fatal fall.

'Certainly not!' Lincoln replied quickly, but Cassie detected a false heartiness in his voice, and an evasiveness in the way he glanced at her and then quickly looked away.

'I wish I had a zap gun that could make Tyler dematerialise like some creature from outer space,' she grumbled. 'Prison's too good for him. He's caused both of us grief for long enough, not to mention the problems he gave your parents.'

Lincoln sighed and reached over to cover Cassie's hand with his. 'Let's just forget about Tyler,' he said.

'He's my problem to handle, and I'll take care of it. OK? Let's talk about more pleasant things, like what kind of wedding we want and where, how we're going to explain everything to Colleen, and...' he paused and grinned at Cassie '...how many brothers and sisters we want to provide her with.'

From behind them came the sound of Willton clearing his throat. Cassie looked quickly around. 'I don't think we're going to be able to keep the news from you,' she said, smiling at the elderly man.

'Willton, you're definitely the exception to my rule to keep our engagement a secret until I return from New York,' Lincoln said. 'I thank you for your help last night,'

'And so do I,' Cassie added. 'You were truly a friend in need.'

Willton beamed. 'I was only trying to perform a service for you both,' he said modestly. 'I hope you'll accept my heartiest congratulations.' He made another little coughing noise. 'I must admit, I forsaw this outcome some time ago.'

'So did I, Willton,' Lincoln said with a mischievous grin. 'But convincing this lovely lady took some time.'

When Willton had gone, Lincoln attacked his breakfast with gusto. 'I'm going to have to keep up my strength,' he said, 'in preparation for raising a horde of happy little Snows. Shall we try to fill this house? My parents tried, and I must admit we had a lot of fun.'

'Get serious!' Cassie cried. 'There are ten bedrooms in this place! Do I look like a mother rabbit to you?'

Their good-natured arguing over that issue continued for several days. It seemed to Cassie that she must have never been so completely happy before. As if a special halo of sunshine were following her, everything she attempted went well.

'My dear, you are going to be a real star,' Ogden Warren gushed after the first week of rehearsals. 'Broadway is going to beckon. I'm sure of it.'

'Let them,' Cassie replied. 'My heart belongs to the Midvale College Shakespeare Festival.'

'And to Lincoln Snow,' Ogden said knowingly. 'I'm afraid when he goes back to New York...or is he going back?'

Cassie shrugged. 'I'm not sure. He hasn't told me.'

'Why is it I doubt that?' Ogden asked. 'Well, never mind. Tell old Link that if he stays we'll get him on the stage too, one day soon. Use the children as well. Keep the family together, eh, what? Don't look so put out, Cassie love. I can tell a wedding's in the offing. You're glowing like a candle all the time.'

Cassie's mother also guessed the truth.

'She can see right through me,' Cassie told Lincoln later when she joined him in the library for after-dinner coffee. 'She always could. There was no use denying it. I didn't admit anything to Oggie, though. I told him to keep his guesses to himself and I'd tell him as soon as there was any truth to them.'

'No harm done, I suppose,' Lincoln said distractedly. 'Now , where the devil did I put that list? Oh, here it is.' He gave Cassie a desperate look. 'You have no idea how I wish I didn't have to go through this next couple of weeks. Please ignore me if I'm short-tempered. I've got to plan for a couple of dozen meetings, none of which I want to attend. Would you mind reading Colleen her bedtime story tonight? I'm not in the mood for *Peter Rabbit*.'

'No, I wouldn't mind at all,' Cassie replied. She got up and gave Lincoln a kiss on the top of his head. 'See you later,' she said, but he was already concentrating on a page of figures and seemed not to hear her. If that was the way his job on Wall Street had affected him, Cassie mused, it wasn't entirely surprising that passionate Magda had got out of hand. But, when later that evening she looked in on Lincoln again, he turned off his computer and held out his arms to her.

'Sorry I was so distracted earlier,' he said, taking her on to his lap and kissing her lovingly. 'Mmm, lovely. Let's go to bed and see how much you can distract me now.'

'I can drive you wild,' Cassie promised. 'I'm already there myself.'

For the next week Lincoln spent most of his daytime hours hunched over his computer keyboard, but stopped at dinnertime and turned his attention to Cassie and Colleen. Cassie took the opportunity to take Colleen to her parents' farm whenever her rehearsal schedule permitted. Once she knew of the wedding plans, Cassie's mother provided not only the a new grandmother for Colleen but also brought in some other children Colleen's age for the little girl to play with.

'She's hardly ever played with other children,' Mrs Lindstrom said anxiously, before the first encounter. 'She's so self-conscious about her brace.'

'Not to worry,' Cassie said comfortingly. 'The girl she's meeting has a brother who wears one. I have hopes that will make it easier.'

To Cassie's delight, Colleen was only nervous before she met Miranda Detweiler. The two children were both doll-lovers, and as soon as they began comparing notes on that subject, anything but their mutual game was forgotten. By the end of the afternoon, Colleen was begging to be allowed to play with Miranda again, 'real soon.'

'That worked out even better than I'd hoped,' Cassie's mother commented.

'It certainly did,' Cassie agreed. 'Everything's been going so well for me lately that I'm getting jittery. I think it's mostly because Lincoln is so tied up in knots over his trip to New York. He hates everything about that trip, but he's got to go.'

'Duties are sometimes like that,' Mrs Lewis said with an understanding nod. 'But cheer up, it will soon be over.'

'It can't end soon enough for me,' Cassie said. 'Lincoln was doing pretty well until a few days ago. Then, he got a whole truckload of boxes of things from his apartment in New York. He had them taken to a big room in the old carriage house and spent a day going through them. I guess that got him behind on his other work, because he's hardly said a word to anyone since. He just sits in there and types like mad for a while and then puffs on one of those awful cigars of his and stares at an ugly brass urn that he found. I'm beginning to wonder if there's an evil genie inside it.'

'There could be some unpleasant memories connected with it, or stored in some of those boxes he went through,' Mrs Lewis said. 'From what you've told me, he didn't have a very happy life there.'

'I'm sure that's part of it,' Cassie said with a sigh. 'Too bad he didn't just burn all of that stuff.'

'You can't really burn memories,' Mrs Lewis said. 'When did you say Lincoln is leaving?'

'Next Monday morning,' Cassie replied. 'He's got four days of business meetings, then the meeting with Tyler and his lawyers. He plans to be back on Saturday in time for the dress rehearsal of *Macbeth*.'

'Why don't you and Colleen stay over here while he's gone? We'd love to have you, and I'm sure Mrs Lindstrom would be glad to have a few days off.'

'You wouldn't see much of me,' Cassie said with a frown. 'Ogden's idea of a rehearsal schedule next week is likely to be noon to midnight.'

'Even more reason to come here,' Mrs Lewis said. 'I don't like the idea of you going home to that big lonely place at midnight.'

'I'll let you know,' Cassie said. She was going to suggest the idea to Lincoln that night, but he was already asleep when she got home and did not even stir when she slipped into bed. In the morning, he was gone when she awoke. 'Are you avoiding me?' she asked, pursuing the smell of his cigar smoke into the library.

'No,' he replied without looking up. 'I'm busy.'

'Well, give me your attention for a darned minute!' Cassie snapped. 'Would it meet with Your Highness's approval if Colleen and I stayed at my parents' while you're gone?'

Lincoln glanced at Cassie for a moment and then nodded. 'I was going to suggest it,' he said before turning back to his work.

'Then why didn't you?' Cassie said loudly. 'Darn it all, Lincoln, I am not built to take this kind of neglect. If you really love me, you can put me at the top of your list of priorities once in a while, no matter how much work you have to do. You're acting like the zombie I found when I first got here.'

'I feel like it,' Lincoln replied. He reached out and took hold of Cassie's hand. 'I'm sorry,' he said. 'I've got some of the same things on my mind as I did then. I thought it was over, but...' He shook his head despairingly. 'Something brought it back.' He gave Cassie the most fleeting of smiles. 'I'll be all right,' he said. 'I just have to think things through.'

'Think things through!' Cassie exploded. 'For Pete's sake, Lincoln, talk to me. I'm going to be your wife, remember?'

'Don't yell at me, Cassie, I'm doing the best that I can,' Lincoln said, his face suddenly so bleak and tired-looking that her heart instantly went out to him.

'I'm sorry,' she said, putting her arm around him and pressing her cheek against his. 'It's just that I'm so worried about you. You haven't been yourself at all the past few days. Ever since those boxes came from your apartment. Does what's worrying you have something to do with those or with that thing?' She pointed to the urn.

Lincoln nodded. 'I'll ... I'll tell you before I go,' he said. 'Can you be patient until then?'

'I'll do my best,' Cassie replied.

If Cassie had not had her rehearsals to distract her for the rest of the week, she was sure she would have gone as mad as Lady Macbeth. Watching Lincoln struggling with his inner turmoil without trying to make him talk about it nearly drove her crazy.

'Your Kate is getting a little too edgy,' Ogden commented. 'She's apt to scare poor Petruchio right out of his shorts. Everything all right with Lincoln?'

'Just fine,' Cassie lied, managing a sweet smile. 'I'll try to smooth Kate out next time.'

She tried smiling sweetly at Lincoln, also, but he seemed so involved in his own thoughts that he did not notice. Even at night the only thing he responded to was a massage that helped relieve the tension that had turned his muscles to painful knots.

On Sunday, the day before Lincoln was to leave, Cassie's nerves were frayed to the breaking-point. He had still told her nothing. The telephone seemed to be ringing constantly. By late afternoon, the door to Lincoln's office remained closed, a 'Do Not Disturb' sign hung over the doorknob. From the sofa in the salon where Cassie had curled up with a book she was not reading, she noticed Willton going in and out of Lincoln's office frequently.

'Do you suppose, Willton,' Cassie finally asked irritably, 'that Lincoln could take a few minutes to talk to me some time today?'

'I'm sure he will in a little while, Miss Cassandra,' Willton replied. 'There have been a great many last-minute details to attend to.'

When another half-hour went by, and Lincoln's door had still not opened, Cassie was about to go and demand that he let her in. This was, she thought, no way to treat the woman he supposedly loved! She had just got to her feet when the door finally opened.

'Good. You're right here,' Lincoln said, spotting her. 'Come on in. I want to talk to you.'

It's about time, Cassie thought, but she did not say it aloud. Lincoln's face was so tense and bleak that she hardly recognised him as the man who could look so warm and loving that it set her heart skipping with joy. 'Are you all right?' she asked, pausing beside him at the door to the office.

'I'm fine,' he replied, giving her a fleeting smile and dropping a perfunctory kiss on her forehead. He closed the door and gestured towards a chair next to his desk. 'Sit down.'

Cassie sat and studied Lincoln while he returned to his own chair. His rumpled white shirt was open almost to the waist, the sleeves pushed up above his elbows. His hair, which he had finally had trimmed, was in wild disarray from his habit of combing his fingers through it while he thought. The lines about his eyes were deep with fatigue, and the scar below his right cheekbone, the only one still prominent, looked aggravated from absent-minded rubbing. He picked up a still burning cigar from his ashtray, glanced at Cassie, and then stubbed it out. He sighed deeply.

'Where shall I begin?' he said, almost as if talking to himself.

'How about at the beginning?' Cassie suggested. 'It's driving me insane to see you so unhappy, and have you shut me out like this. It's not fair! I want to share your life, not the pieces you happen to feel like giving me. I want you to tell me right now exactly what it was that happened that night that you fell to make you so depressed, and what's happened now to bring it back. And don't leave anything out!'

For a long time, Lincoln did not reply. At last he sighed again. 'All right, Cassie,' he said. He folded his hands on the desk in front of him and stared at them as he spoke. 'The night that I fell,' he said softly, in a strangely flat voice, 'Tyler and I had had an argument over the usual thing, money, which degenerated into some stupid name-calling when I reminded him of some of his other shortcomings. I went out to the roof garden to cool off. Tyler came out, wanting to keep up the fight. When I turned my back on him, he told me that he'd had enough of me. He was going to get rid of me and inherit everything. I told him not to be foolish. First of all, he was unlikely to get away with murder, and secondly, he wouldn't inherit anything since I'd cut him out of my will after Magda died. Apparently, something snapped when I told him that, because he started yelling a stream of obscenities and saying he'd kill me anyway because he hated me. I turned around just in time to see him coming at me with this urn from the garden in his hand, raised like a weapon.'

Lincoln looked at the urn, his face still impassive. 'I dodged a little bit in the time I had, and the edge of that square base hit the top of my head. There's still some of my hair and scalp embedded in it...right there.' He pointed to one of the sides of the base. 'If the corner had hit me instead...' Lincoln paused for a moment, his mouth pursed in a tight line, then went on. 'I guess my head's pretty hard, since it didn't knock me out. All it did was make me see everything through a white-hot anger that wiped everything from my mind but a desire to kill Tyler before he killed me. I kicked the urn from his hand and then grabbed him by the throat and shook him as if he were a small toy. He grabbed my throat, too, but I was stronger, and in a few minutes I had the upper hand. I was all set to throw him over the railing when it hit me what I was doing. I pushed him away from me, but in doing so lost my balance and fell backwards against the railing, which gave way. Fortunately, I had the presence of mind to put my arm in front of my eyes or I'd probably be blind now. I was unconscious, of course, after I landed, but when I came to, in the hospital, I remembered the whole scene vividly, over and over, like a tape loop that wouldn't stop.'

Lincoln looked briefly at Cassie and then down at his hands again. Cassie said nothing, watching him closely for some clue to his emotions. There was nothing but the same, tightly controlled tension.

'It was a horrifying experience, in every way,' Lincoln said slowly, 'but what was most troubling to me was not the fact that Tyler wanted me dead, which did not surprise me, nor the fall itself. It was the fact that I was capable of such hatred that the idea of killing Tyler was almost pleasant. Not almost. At the time, it was pleasant.' Lincoln looked up at Cassie. Now there was a bright intensity in his eyes, a deep note of emotion in his voice. 'I didn't want to be that kind of a person. I wanted to be able to forgive, and try to understand, no matter what someone did. I discovered a person inside me who was not like that, a person I couldn't accept. I wondered when he would try to get out again. With Tyler, it was a double problem. I felt guilty for not having done more to change his ways, and frightened that he might provoke me again.

'Then you came into my life, with your strong emotions, and your ability to express them. Your story of Tyler and your baby rabbit helped me to see that my own reaction was not so unique. Even though you were only a child when it happened, you sensed something deeply wrong with Tyler. I began to see that it was likely that Tyler had had some deep-seated problems all his life. Maybe it all started when his

parents died. I don't know. I guess we'll never know.
But we'd all tried—professionals had tried—everyone
had done the best they could to help him, in spite of
his ugly behaviour. No one was really to blame for
failing him.

'When he attacked you, I realised how really
dangerous he is. I thought of trying to charge him
with attemped murder, but was afraid it would be difficult to prove, since it would be his word against mine
and I would be changing my story. I didn't think of
the urn then, except as a source of fingerprints, and
there could be plenty of other reasons for Tyler's fingerprints being on it. I never thought of how hard he
had hit me and the fact that part of my head would
have clung to it until I looked at it the other day. It's
obvious, even with a small magnifying glass. Besides,
until two days ago I was still very reluctant to take
such a step. I was content with having Tyler elim-
inated as a problem to us for some time, and probably
put in a facility where he would get some psycho-
logical help as well. That was before I opened the
boxes in which Magda's clothing had been packed
away. Pandora's boxes, as it turned out.'

Cassie could keep silent no longer. 'What else did
you find?' she cried. 'What has changed?'

'I found evidence,' Lincoln said slowly, obviously
having difficulty now controlling his emotions, 'that
Tyler not only tried to kill me, but that he did, deliberately, force Magda to have sex with him, with full
knowledge that it might lead to her death as well as
that of the child she was carrying. She had a condition called . . .' Lincoln looked at Cassie pleadingly.

'Placenta previa,' Cassie said.

Lincoln nodded, took a deep breath and went on. 'Magda had a beautiful green velvet robe. In the pocket of that robe, I found a diary that I never knew she kept. It clearly describes the course of her relationship with Tyler, how he became more and more sadistic, until...' Lincoln stopped and buried his face in his hands for a moment. 'Until,' he went on hoarsely, 'she begged him to leave her alone. When he wouldn't she managed to put him off long enough to make sure that I got her pregnant, thinking that Tyler would lose interest then. From the dates in the diary, it's clear that Colleen is mine, and I either misunderstood or didn't remember what she told me correctly. Instead of losing interest, Tyler got rough and demanded that Magda get rid of the child. He told her he was going to take care of me as soon as he got a gun, and then she and Tyler would have everything. The poor woman was beside herself, afraid to come to me, terrified of Tyler. He somehow got a gun and made wild, elaborate plans to kill me. When Magda tried to take the gun from him, he forced her to sit all one night when I was gone with the gun at her head. Then, the night before I returned home and found them, he forced her to tell the servants to leave the next day. She managed to scribble a few notes that night. Tyler was going to... to rape her the next day. He told her he was tired of her excuses and hoped that she was right that it would kill her, since she told him that she loved me, not him. Then he was going to lie in wait for me. Her last words were, "Dear heaven, how I wish Lincoln were here now to stop this insanity!"'

Lincoln closed his eyes, a tear edging out from the corner of each eye. 'Magda. Colleen. Tyler. How could I have been so wrong about so many things?' he asked hoarsely.

'You don't have a crystal ball, my love,' Cassie answered softly. 'With everyone trying to deceive you, and your gentle, trusting heart, it's not so surprising. It's not surprising at all.'

Lincoln gave Cassie a weary smile. 'Thank you. Fortunately when Magda died I did truthfully report the circumstances that led to her haemorrhaging, mostly because I didn't want the doctors to think I was at fault. An affair with my nephew, I said. Now I'm faced with making the charges against Tyler, and making very sure that they stick. He's far more dangerous than I ever dreamed. I'm probably lucky to still be here myself, as erratic as he is. I think only my willingness to dispense money and his fear that I might know something incriminating has kept him from trying something in the past. He has a morbid fear of being imprisoned.'

'Oh, Lincoln, do be careful,' Cassie said, suddenly realising that he was soon going to be facing Tyler once more. 'Don't ever be alone with Tyler.'

'I don't plan to be,' Lincoln assured her. He stood up and held out his arms to Cassie, then silently folded her close as she moved to put her arms around him. He held her tightly for a long time, then took her chin in his hand and lifted her face to his. 'I don't know how long I'll be away now,' he said, his eyes so sad that Cassie felt as if her heart would burst with the sorrow she felt with him. 'I've got to stay in New York until I'm sure that Tyler isn't going to be free to come here again. I have hopes he won't be able to be out on bail . . .'

'But if he is, you'll have to wait for the trial. That could be months!' Cassie cried. 'And all the while I'll be here, worried about you night and day.'

'I don't think that will happen,' Lincoln said comfortingly. 'But I do think that we should put off our wedding until after the trial. It's apt to be one of the kind the scandal sheets love, about the sordid lives of the rich. I don't want you involved.'

'Oh, you don't?' Cassie pulled back and frowned at Lincoln. 'I thought I'd be signing up for better or for worse. I want to be with you, to help you. You're going to be going through something that's terribly traumatic for you. Deep inside, you still wish it didn't have to be the way it does. If you can't let me share it . . .'

Lincoln smiled gently and brushed Cassie's hair back from her forehead before he kissed it tenderly. 'There's no point in our starting off our marriage with something that's definitely worse. You have your work with the Festival to keep you busy. I'll call you and come and see you as often as I can manage. I'm going to close up Oak Hill while I'm gone and take Willton and Colleen and Mrs Lindstrom with me. In fact, I'm sending Colleen and Mrs Lindstrom on ahead tonight. I've rented an apartment in a nice, secure building, so you needn't be worried about me. I'm sure your parents will be glad to have you with them while I'm gone, and then, when I get back, we can get married and start off with everything perfect.' He started to lower his head to kiss Cassie's lips.

'No! Stop treating me like a child.' Cassie pushed him away, hot tears of anger welling in her eyes. 'You don't really love me,' she said, backing away from him. 'You don't really understand how I feel, as you claimed you do. First you suffer for days without telling me anything, never caring that I'm suffering too, watching you. Now, you go and make all of these plans without ever consulting me once to see if they're what I want. Well, they're not what I want. Not at all!'

'Cassie, be reasonable,' Lincoln said sternly. 'I do love you. I'm not leaving forever. I still want to marry you. I just don't want you to be saddled immediately with a mass of problems that are not of your making. I'm apt to be tense and short-tempered and unreasonable part of the time and confused and unhappy the rest of it. You've seen enough of that side of me. When we marry, I want to be the kind of man you can count on through thick and thin to be strong and solid and reliable.'

'I never said I wanted you to be different from the way you are. I only want you to talk to me instead of keeping everything inside!' But, Cassie noted, there was already something different about Lincoln. Something in that stubbornly intractable set of his jaw as he silently listened to her reminded her of her father. Frustrated, she went on, 'I don't want someone who thinks he's calm and reasonable all of the time. I fell in love with a passionate, loving man who brought warmth and sunshine into my life, not calm, cold logic. If all I'm going to get is what's left after you've filtered the life out of everything you feel, then I don't want it! I'll never know what's going on inside of your head. Even now I'm not sure you've told me everything. How do I know it isn't only what you think I should hear?'

'You don't,' Lincoln replied. 'You have to trust me, and remember that I love you.'

Cassie shook her head. 'I don't know if I can do that, Lincoln. Not after the way you've treated me this past week or two.' She started towards the door. 'I'm sorry about everything. You've been through so much, it's probably not your fault. I hope you get your life straightened out so that you can be happy with someone. I think I'll go home to my parents' house now. It will only take a few minutes to pack.'

Lincoln nodded, his face still impassive. 'That might be best,' he said, then turned to answer his ringing telephone. 'Yes?' he answered. He picked up a pen. 'When?'

I was right. He doesn't care, Cassie thought, a terrible anguish filling her. He wasn't even listening to what I said. She put her hand on the doorknob and turned it. 'Goodbye, Lincoln,' she whispered, and fled across the foyer and up the stairs. She flung her clothing helter-skelter into her suitcases, scarcely able to see through the tears that streamed down her cheeks. A short time later, she dashed down the stairs and out through the huge front door of Oak Hill as fast as she could go. In less than five more minutes she was back in her old room at the Lewis farm, lying sobbing into the pillow on the same bed where so many years before she had penned the words, 'I am in love with Lincoln Snow. I shall love him forever.' Only now, she knew, no matter what she had told Lincoln, those words were true.

CHAPTER TEN

THERE was a tap on the door of Cassie's bedroom.

'Go away,' she sobbed.

The door opened anyway and moments later Cassie felt her mother sit down on the bed beside her and her mother's gentle hand caress her shoulders. 'Want to talk about it?' her mother asked after a few minutes. When Cassie turned her head, she saw her mother's hand, holding out a handful of Kleenex. Cassie took them and sat up.

'It's nothing new,' Cassie said bitterly, once she had dried her tears. 'I'm an idiot. I got angry with Lincoln when I should have been kind and gentle instead. Now I've lost him.' She felt a new tear start down alongside her nose and brushed it angrily away. 'I don't think he'll ever want anything to do with me again.'

Cassie's mother sighed. 'Come on into the kitchen and have some coffee. Things will look better when you've had some time to calm down.'

'I doubt it,' Cassie said, but she followed her mother into the familiar, warm room where she had talked out so many of her problems before. Her mother poured them both a cup of coffee and then sat down opposite her.

'What makes you so positive that Lincoln won't be willing to patch things up?' she asked. 'What did you argue about that's so serious you can't reach a compromise? Life is full of compromises, you know.'

'I wish you'd reminded me about that yesterday,' Cassie said bitterly. 'It's all my fault. I'm the one who said we were through, and all because Lincoln wants to save me from having to go through the next few weeks with him. It's going to be a terribly sordid mess.' She looked at her mother. 'Tyler's probably going to prison for murder,' she said. 'Lincoln found some things in those boxes...' She choked to a stop and buried her face in her hands.

'Murder? Good heavens, that must have been a shock to Lincoln, even though I know Tyler's been a problem to the Snows all of his life.'

'It was a terrible shock,' Cassie said. 'And he found out that he'd been wrong...' She shook her head. The details of Tyler and Magda's sordid affair were not something Lincoln would want her to share, even with her mother. 'Oh, why am I so dumb? Just because he didn't want to share his misery with me...'

Cassie's mother sighed. 'I'm afraid I know how you feel only too well. Your father's never been one to express his emotions very well, either. I just have to wait until he's ready. It does no good to rant and rave. I found that out years ago. But, in between, he's a kind and gentle man, as you've probably noticed. And, as you may not know...' Mrs Lewis paused and smiled '...a very passionate and loving man.'

Cassie stared at her mother. 'N-no, I didn't know. I guess he and Lincoln are more alike than I thought.' She stared into space, suddenly remembering the little smiles and caresses her parents sometimes exchanged, the odd times when they both would suddenly be so tired that they had to take a nap. 'I'm afraid I'm not very observant,' she muttered, taking another swallow of coffee. 'Nothing like learning the hard way, is there?'

'It's sometimes the only way,' her mother replied. 'I wouldn't give up on Lincoln, though, in spite of what you may have said to him. You may have to eat some crow later, but——'

'You know what I said that was really stupid?' Cassie interrupted. 'I told Lincoln that I didn't want him to change, and then I told him that I wanted him to talk to me when he didn't feel like talking! I wasn't even listening to myself!'

Mrs Lewis smiled. 'That's not so unusual. People do that all the time. You'll be all right, Cassie, and so will Lincoln. You love each other. That's obvious. It takes time to iron out all of the differences and make a marriage work. It's never easy, no matter what any fairy-tale may say about living happily ever after.'

Cassie nodded. 'I'd better pray that Lincoln's got better sense than I have.' The telephone rang, and Cassie heard the sound of her father's voice answering it in the living-room. His voice was low and soft like Lincoln's. She had always thought of him as a strong man. Lincoln was strong, too, or he would never have been able to face what he had had to face the past few years without breaking. His emotions were sometimes closer to the surface, but thinking back, Cassie realised that she had always known how her father had felt about things. His expression was more restrained, but it was there none the less.

'Rosemary?' Her father appeared in the kitchen door and beckoned to her mother.

'I'll be right back,' Mrs Lewis said, smiling at Cassie. 'Have some more coffee.' She returned a few minutes later, shaking her head. 'Poor old Seth

Barnhardt's in the hospital with his back again. We've got to feed the dog while he's there. Cora's always so apologetic. You'd think she was asking us to take care of the whole world instead of one tiny dog.'

'She's a good old soul,' Cassie's father said, coming into the kitchen and taking the chair next to Cassie. 'How's my girl?' he asked. 'Having some problems?'

Cassie looked into her father's direct blue eyes and suddenly burst into fresh tears. How could she ever have thought her father was lacking in feeling? There was a world of love and understanding in his eyes. 'I'm the stupidest idiot in the world, that's the problem,' she wailed.

'I doubt that very much,' her father said, putting his arm around her shoulders. 'Dry your tears and let's have some supper.'

'Maybe I should go back and talk to Lincoln,' Cassie said, sniffling back her tears once again. 'I don't want him thinking I'm the world's biggest fool for any longer than necessary.'

'You haven't told me what went wrong,' her father said. 'It might help to get a man's point of view.'

'I suppose it might,' Cassie said, looking at her father apprehensively. She couldn't recall his ever having volunteered such a thing before, but then, she had been away from home so much of the time in recent years. 'It's a long story,' she said, 'but it goes like this.' While her mother served their supper, she sketched out the difficulties that had led to her earlier outburst. 'I was way out of line,' she concluded, 'expecting him to do something he can't do, and then telling him I didn't want him on top of it. I love him. I don't want to lose him.'

'You won't,' her father said positively. 'Your mother went home to her mother three or four times after we were married. I knew she was just upset. I didn't really blame her, because there were times when I knew I'd been hard to live with. Still am sometimes, I guess, but we understand each other now. I try not to let things go too long, and she tries not to nag at me about it. You and Lincoln will work it out, but I wouldn't go running back right away. He's got a heavy load on his mind right now.'

'But he's leaving tomorrow,' Cassie said. 'I won't see him for a long time after that.' She bit her lip. 'If I ever see him again.'

'You'll see him,' her father said. 'He's a fine man. He won't want you to suffer any longer than necessary. As soon as he gets some of his own problems taken care of, he'll be here. I guarantee it.'

'But I don't want him thinking I don't love him to add to his problems,' Cassie protested.

'He knows you love him,' her father said with a smile. 'You don't need to worry about that. Just give him a little breathing space. You'll both feel better.'

'I hope you're right,' Cassie said with a sigh. It seemed a little odd that her father was so sure, but she was willing to trust his judgement. Her own had not been faring very well recently. She smiled at her father and then leaned over and gave his leathery cheek a quick kiss. 'How about putting me to work on some chores in the morning? That will help me keep my mind off of my troubles.'

'Glad to,' he replied. 'That way I can get finished in time to come and watch your play-acting. Your mother's been trying to get me to come along and see what a star you are.'

'That's a great idea,' Cassie agreed. 'You'll love watching Oggie Warren playing the great director, too.'

Cassie felt more light-hearted than she would have thought possible when she went to bed that night. She sent a grateful thanks to whomever had provided her with such wonderful parents and a fervent wish that Lincoln could be feeling a little more calm and relaxed also, then went to sleep and slept the whole night through without waking. It was barely getting light when a firm knock on her door awakened her.

'Chore time,' said her father's voice.

'Be right there,' Cassie said, suppressing a desire to groan and turn over and go back to sleep. She got up and put on her oldest jeans and a sweatshirt against the morning chill and quickly joined her father in the kitchen for breakfast. They had just finished breakfast and stepped out on to the back porch, when the distant wail of a siren caught Cassie's attention. 'Must have been an accident,' she said.

Her father listened, then frowned. 'Maybe,' he said.

The sound came closer and closer.

'Can someone we know have been hurt?' Cassie wondered aloud. Farming was a dangerous occupation, and more often than she cared to remember one of their neighbours had been injured. Almost automatically, she and her father stepped down from the porch and walked to the side of the house where they could see the road that ran in front of the Lewis farm. An ambulance, its lights flashing, was coming towards them from Midvale. Suddenly Cassie felt a cold chill, as if a huge, icy hand had wrapped its claw-like fingers around her entire body. Almost simultaneously, a few hundred feet short of the Lewises' farm, the ambulance screeched into the turn down the drive to Oak Hill. She clutched at her father's arm, feeling sick and dizzy. 'What's happened?' Cassie cried, looking at her father with wide, frightened eyes. 'I've got to go...'

'Whoa, there,' her father said, taking hold of Cassie's arm before she could even move. 'Just stay calm. Someone will call and let us know when to come.'

Cassie stared at her father. 'You know something, don't you?' she said. 'What is it? What's going on?' A face with cold, cruel eyes flashed through her memory. Tyler! 'Is it Tyler? Did he come back...to get Lincoln?'

'Let's go inside,' her father said calmly. 'I'll tell you what I know.'

'No!' Cassie shook her head. 'I've got to go. Now!' She wrenched herself free of her father's grasp and ran towards the Oak Hill road, ignoring her father's cries of, 'Cassie! Come back here! It may not be safe.' She ran full tilt, gasping for breath but willing her feet to keep flying. Lincoln might be hurt! Lincoln might need her! She reached the edge of the courtyard at Oak Hill in time to see a young man in medical garb open the huge door and hold it while two other paramedics carried out a stretcher on which lay a sheet-covered body. She ran up to the men. 'What? Who?' she gasped, pointing at the stretcher, her leaden legs feeling wobbly beneath her. When the man did not answer, she reached over and jerked the sheet back, her heart in her throat.

It was Tyler. 'Lincoln!' she screamed. 'Where's Lincoln?'

'Cassie!'

Cassie turned her head. There, standing in the doorway, stood Lincoln, a deputy sheriff in his khaki uniform beside him.

'Come here, Cassie,' Lincoln ordered. He beckoned to her and then turned his attention to the officer.

Cassie glanced once more at the stretcher, now disappearing into the ambulance, and then moved like a sleep-walker towards Lincoln.

'I'm sorry it turned out that way, sir,' the deputy was saying. 'In a situation like that, you can't shoot to wound.'

'I know,' Lincoln replied, putting a hand on the man's shoulder. 'You did what you had to do. I appreciate your courage and skill.'

Lincoln put out his arm and caught Cassie as she came to him, pulling her against his side in a comforting embrace. He smiled briefly at her upturned face and then went on talking to the deputy about what he would have to do to make his report. Cassie stared at Lincoln. She felt as if she were seeing him for the first time. He looked so strong. So solid. He was still wearing the same rumpled shirt as the night before, but his face no longer bore the lines of terrible tension that had seemed so permanent a part of him in the past few weeks. He looked, Cassie thought, a little sad, but very relieved. Past him, bending over something on the floor of the huge foyer, she could see Willton. Quietly, she freed herself from Lincoln's arm and went to see what he was doing.

The old man was crouched awkwardly on one knee beside a bucket of water, rapidly sponging up the remains of a pool of blood.

'Let me help,' Cassie said, dropping to one knee beside him and holding out her hand for the sponge. 'You can tell me what happened. Lincoln's busy.'

Willton nodded gratefully and handed her the sponge, then pushed his arthritic joints back to a standing position. 'There's not much to tell, Miss Cassandra,' he said. 'Mr Scofield, the deputy, and Mr Snow were waiting in the salon. When Mr Tyler arrived, Mr Scofield took up a position where he could see without being seen. I let Mr Tyler in. He demanded to know where everyone was. Actually...' Willton cleared his throat uncomfortably '...he asked if you and Mr Snow were still in bed. Before I could answer, Mr Snow came from the direction of his office, and I moved out of the way very quickly as I had been instructed. Mr Snow said hello to Mr Tyler, told him that he'd been expecting him, and suggested that he not be foolish, that he give himself up before anyone got hurt. Mr Tyler made some—er—obscene remarks and reached for the gun which was protruding from his pocket. At that point, Mr Scofield told him to freeze. When he did not, Mr Scofield opened fire. That was...the end of it.'

Cassie slowly wiped up a last speck of blood and dropped the sponge into the bucket. Lincoln had known Tyler was coming! She stood up and looked towards the open door. Lincoln had stepped outside to say a last word to the departing deputy. He gave a farewell salute and then turned and walked briskly back into the house, tall and straight, his head held high.

'You knew!' Cassie said accusingly, staring at him and shaking her head. 'You knew Tyler was coming and you didn't tell me. You told my father, but you didn't tell me!'

'Of course I didn't,' Lincoln replied, stopping in front of her. 'I didn't want you worried, and I didn't want you in the way. If you hadn't gone scurrying home on your own last night, your father was going to have to invent a reason to get you there.' A glint of mischief sparkled in his eyes. 'That was very good timing on your part, Cassie.'

'Good timing!' Cassie spluttered. 'I didn't . . .' She choked to a stop. This was no time to be yelling at Lincoln. He had just gone through something that he must have been dreading might happen. Cassie put her hands on his shoulders. 'I'm sorry, Lincoln,' she said softly. 'It must have been awful for you. It must still be.'

Lincoln nodded and slipped his arms around her. 'It is, but it's nothing compared to the way I would have felt if anything had happened to you. That I couldn't have borne.' He smiled, his eyes misty. 'I love you so much, Cassie,' he said, then crushed her to him, the sound of a strangled sob coming from his throat. He held very still, and Cassie could feel the heavy pounding of his heart as he fought to regain control of his emotions. At last he raised his head. 'I suppose you want to hear the whole story,' he said with a teasing little smile.

'When you're ready to tell me,' she replied. 'Willton told me what happened here.'

'I'll tell you now,' Lincoln said, 'but let's go upstairs and lie down while I do. I didn't get any sleep last night.' He took hold of Cassie's arm, smiling down at her, then stopped. 'Kiss me first,' he said. 'I need the strength to get up those stairs.'

For a moment, Cassie stood transfixed, her heart skipping with joy before her mind could absorb the meaning of what Lincoln had been saying. After everything that had happened, Lincoln wanted her to kiss him? To stay with him? He didn't want to be left alone to brood? Suddenly, a joyous smile broke across her face and she flung her arms around him. Her father was right. Lincoln did understand. 'Oh, Lincoln! I love you so much,' she said, clinging to him tightly, her face buried against his neck. 'Please forgive me for being such a shrew last night. It was just that I want so much to be a part of everything that's you. I want to comfort you, and help you, but I know now——'

'Be quiet and kiss me. Then I'll forgive you,' Lincoln said.

Cassie raised her head and looked at him. In his eyes were all the warmth and love that she could ever dream of having, in the soft, gentle lips that touched hers, every promise of happiness that she could want. She opened her mouth to his increasingly passionate kiss, letting all of the doubts and fears of recent days fly wordlessly away.

'Now am I forgiven?' Cassie asked, when Lincoln at last raised his head and smiled at her adoringly.

'There was never anything to forgive,' he replied. 'You were simply being yourself, responding to what had been a terribly stressful time for both of us. I hated having to shut you out, but there was no way… Let's go upstairs. I'm too tired to explain it all standing here.'

They climbed the stairs to their room together, flung back the covers, then stretched out with Cassie nestled in the curve of Lincoln's shoulder. Lincoln heaved a heavy sigh.

'Thank goodness you're here with me and safe,' he said. 'It's a grim sort of happiness, but a great relief to know that I won't have to worry about that any more.' He kissed Cassie's forehead and caressed her back soothingly. 'There's not much to tell you, besides what you already know,' he said. 'I don't know all the details myself yet. What I do know is this: yesterday morning I got a call from the detectives in New York whom I've been employing to keep track of Tyler. An informant had told them that Tyler had been in a bar Saturday night, boasting to someone that he was coming back here to kill you because you were the reason for all of his troubles.'

'Good lord!' Cassie cried, a shiver going through her. 'Where did he ever get that idea?'

'I don't know,' Lincoln replied, holding her tighter and kissing her again. 'My guess is that he felt that if I hadn't fallen in love with you, things would have gone on as they had before, once I was well. He may have blamed you for the fact that I was getting tough with him, and he may even have had some idea that the law was about to come into the picture because you disliked him so much. It makes some kind of warped sense, I guess.'

'I suppose so,' Cassie agreed with a sigh. She tugged Lincoln's shirt loose and began running her hand up and down his bare back.

'Mmm,' Lincoln murmured contentedly. 'That feels heavenly. Anyway, I definitely wasn't going to tell you that and frighten you. Then, only a couple of hours later, I got another call. Tyler had stolen a car and then shot a policeman who tried to apprehend him.

He was heading west. I made arrangements to send Colleen and Mrs Lindstrom to a hotel in Midvale and sent the rest of the staff home late yesterday afternoon. Willton refused to leave, so I included him in my plans. After that, it was like tracking the path of any fugitive, except that we knew pretty well where he was headed. I got one phone call after another. Tyler ran a roadblock in Ohio and injured another policeman in the process. He wrecked the first car and stole another. By the time he hit Indiana, everyone believed me that he was coming here. I managed to convince them to only post the one deputy here with me and let me try to talk him into giving himself up, rather than have a large group waiting to jump him. I'm afraid that would have been a real shoot-out.'

'I think you're right,' Cassie said, tilting her head back and looking into the deep, clear hazel eyes that she loved so dearly. 'I guess it's just as well I didn't know. Thank you for protecting me.' She paused and put on her fiercest frown. 'But don't you ever do that again, Lincoln Snow!'

'Yes, ma'am,' he agreed, pretending to look frightened. Then he laughed. 'Oh, Cassie, we're going to have such a wonderful life together. There's a great empty ache inside me for all the things that might have been if only I had been wiser or more clever in the past, but there's no use trying to fill it with tears.' He leaned forward and kissed Cassie's lips and then tenderly smoothed her hair back with his fingertips. 'I'll fill it with happiness and your love instead.'

'That's a lovely thought,' Cassie said, caressing Lincoln's cheek as he stretched out and moulded her closer against him. 'You have all my love, you know. You always have and you always will.'

'And you have mine,' Lincoln said, gathering Cassie close and cuddling her against him. 'Last night, after you'd gone, I found that what bothered me the most was that you still doubted my love, although I can understand why you might have. I longed to be able to come to you with words that would erase those doubts forever. So, last night, as I was trying to brace myself for Tyler's arrival, I sat down and picked up my old copy of the works of Shakespeare to see if he could help me persuade you. Oggie was right, the man said it all.' Lincoln paused and lifted Cassie's face to his with his hand. 'From *Hamlet*, Act II, scene ii,' he said huskily. '"Doubt thou the stars are fire; Doubt that the sun doth move; Doubt truth to be a liar; But never doubt I love."' He kissed her lips again.

Cassie's eyes were misty. 'I think it's . . . perfectly amazing, that in the midst of all the trauma and turmoil you must have been suffering last night, that you spent time looking through Shakespeare so that you could convince me not to doubt your love.'

Lincoln laughed softly. 'That wasn't what a strong, solid, reliable man would do, was it?'

'It's what the strong, solid, reliable man I love would do,' Cassie replied. She sighed, then slowly began unbuttoning his shirt. 'I suppose you still have to leave for New York right away?'

'I'll go tomorrow, and only stay for a couple of days. Anything that can't get done then will be done by telephone or mail. I can't spare any more time away from my love.' He cleared his throat, then frowned and stayed Cassie's hand.

'What is it?' Cassie asked. Lincoln obviously had something more that he wanted to tell her. 'Come on, now,' she teased. 'I don't want to have to start yelling at you again.'

Lincoln smiled. 'You won't. I'm just so tired that my mind is wandering, and all it wants to wander to is——'

'Let it,' Cassie interrupted.

'All right,' Lincoln said, beginning to explore beneath Cassie's sweater. 'At the same time, I'll tell you that I was hoping . . . that is, I'd like for us to get married as soon as I get back. Somehow, the more I think about waiting until the first of August, the less I like it. You and I belong together as man and wife. Do you suppose that you could fit a small wedding into your schedule?'

'I'll make it fit!' Cassie replied. She paused in her caressing of Lincoln's chest. 'Ogden's taking July the fourth off. Opening night's the fifth. Why don't we get married on the fourth? We can pretend all the fireworks are just for us.'

'That will be great. We'll make our own fireworks,' Lincoln said with a happy smile. A glint of mischief lighted his eyes. 'A lot of fireworks. There are ten bedrooms in this house and I'm not getting any younger.'

'Oh, no! We decided on four at the most. That would be five, counting Colleen.'

'Well, if you're going to be stubborn . . .' Lincoln frowned and stood up, but only long enough to remove the rest of his clothing. He smiled as he watched Cassie doing the same. 'To think that I'm going to be able to watch that for the rest of my life,' he said.

'You're nowhere near as lucky as I,' Cassie said, casting an appreciative glance at Lincoln's well-proportioned body. She lay back and pulled Lincoln down beside her, gazing into the dearest face she had ever known, the gentle, loving face of the man who had captured her heart so many years ago. 'Welcome back to our life,' she whispered in the moment before their lips met and their bodies began to melt together in blissful closeness. 'On our wedding day I'll show you where it all began.'

For a wedding gift, Cassie had the page from her diary framed in gold and gave it to Lincoln on the morning of their wedding day. 'I was fourteen when I wrote that,' she said, 'just after you gave me Monty II.'

'"I am in love with Lincoln Snow. I shall love him forever,"' Lincoln read aloud. He looked at her, his eyes shining with tears of joy. 'I shall love you forever, Cassie,' he said. 'Never doubt my love.'

PENNY JORDAN

Sins and infidelities...
Dreams and obsessions...
Shattering secrets
unfold in...

THE HIDDEN YEARS

SAGE — stunning, sensual and vibrant, she spent a lifetime distancing herself from a past too painful to confront... the mother who seemed to hold her at bay, the father who resented her and the heartache of unfulfilled love. To the world, Sage was independent and invulnerable— but it was a mask she cultivated to hide a desperation she herself couldn't quite understand... until an unforeseen turn of events drew her into the discovery of the hidden years, finally allowing Sage to open her heart to a passion denied for so long.

The Hidden Years—a compelling novel of truth and passion that will unlock the heart and soul of every woman.

AVAILABLE IN OCTOBER!
Watch for your opportunity to complete your Penny Jordan set.
POWER PLAY and SILVER will also be available in October.

HIDDEN-RR

FASHION WHOLE NEW YOU

WIN
CARS, TRIPS, CASH!

HARLEQUIN®
OFFICIAL SWEEPSTAKES
RULES

NO PURCHASE NECESSARY

1. To enter, complete an Official Entry Form or 3" × 5" index card by hand-printing, in plain block letters, your complete name, address, phone number and age, and mailing it to: Harlequin Fashion A Whole New You Sweepstakes, P.O. Box 9056, Buffalo, NY 14269-9056.

   No responsibility is assumed for lost, late or misdirected mail. Entries must be sent separately with first class postage affixed, and be received no later than December 31, 1991 for eligibility.

2. Winners will be selected by D.L. Blair, Inc., an independent judging organization whose decisions are final, in random drawings to be held on January 30, 1992 in Blair, NE at 10:00 a.m. from among all eligible entries received.

3. The prizes to be awarded and their approximate retail values are as follows: Grand Prize — A brand-new Mercury Sable LS plus a trip for two (2) to Paris, including round-trip air transportation, six (6) nights hotel accommodation, a $1,400 meal/spending money stipend and $2,000 cash toward a new fashion wardrobe (approximate value: $28,000) or $15,000 cash; two (2) Second Prizes — A trip to Paris, including round-trip air transportation, six (6) nights hotel accommodation, a $1,400 meal/spending money stipend and $2,000 cash toward a new fashion wardrobe (approximate value: $11,000) or $5,000 cash; three (3) Third Prizes — $2,000 cash toward a new fashion wardrobe. All prizes are valued in U.S. currency. Travel award air transportation is from the commercial airport nearest winner's home. Travel is subject to space and accommodation availability, and must be completed by June 30, 1993. Sweepstakes offer is open to residents of the U.S. and Canada who are 21 years of age or older as of December 31, 1991, except residents of Puerto Rico, employees and immediate family members of Torstar Corp., its affiliates, subsidiaries, and all agencies, entities and persons connected with the use, marketing, or conduct of this sweepstakes. All federal, state, provincial, municipal and local laws apply. Offer void wherever prohibited by law. Taxes and/or duties, applicable registration and licensing fees, are the sole responsibility of the winners. Any litigation within the province of Quebec respecting the conduct and awarding of a prize may be submitted to the Régie des loteries et courses du Québec. All prizes will be awarded; winners will be notified by mail. No substitution of prizes is permitted.

4. Potential winners must sign and return any required Affidavit of Eligibility/Release of Liability within 30 days of notification. In the event of noncompliance within this time period, the prize may be awarded to an alternate winner. Any prize or prize notification returned as undeliverable may result in the awarding of that prize to an alternate winner. By acceptance of their prize, winners consent to use of their names, photographs or their likenesses for purposes of advertising, trade and promotion on behalf of Torstar Corp. without further compensation. Canadian winners must correctly answer a time-limited arithmetical question in order to be awarded a prize.

5. For a list of winners (available after 3/31/92), send a separate stamped, self-addressed envelope to: Harlequin Fashion A Whole New You Sweepstakes, P.O. Box 4694, Blair, NE 68009.

PREMIUM OFFER TERMS

To receive your gift, complete the Offer Certificate according to directions. Be certain to enclose the required number of "Fashion A Whole New You" proofs of product purchase (which are found on the last page of every specially marked "Fashion A Whole New You" Harlequin or Silhouette romance novel). Requests must be received no later than December 31, 1991. Limit: four (4) gifts per name, family, group, organization or address. Items depicted are for illustrative purposes only and may not be exactly as shown. Please allow 6 to 8 weeks for receipt of order. Offer good while quantities of gifts last. In the event an ordered gift is no longer available, you will receive a free, previously unpublished Harlequin or Silhouette book for every proof of purchase you have submitted with your request, plus a refund of the postage and handling charge you have included. Offer good in the U.S. and Canada only.

HOFW-SWPR

HARLEQUIN® OFFICIAL SWEEPSTAKES ENTRY FORM

4-FWHRS-2

Complete and return this Entry Form immediately – the more entries you submit, the better your chances of winning!

- Entries must be received by **December 31, 1991**.
- A Random draw will take place on **January 30, 1992**.
- No purchase necessary.

Yes, I want to win a FASHION A WHOLE NEW YOU Classic and Romantic prize from Harlequin:

Name _____ Telephone _____ Age _____

Address _____

City _____ State _____ Zip _____

Return Entries to: **Harlequin FASHION A WHOLE NEW YOU,**
P.O. Box 9056, Buffalo, NY 14269-9056   © 1991 Harlequin Enterprises Limited

PREMIUM OFFER

To receive your free gift, send us the required number of proofs-of-purchase from any specially marked FASHION A WHOLE NEW YOU Harlequin or Silhouette Book with the Offer Certificate properly completed, plus a check or money order (do not send cash) to cover postage and handling payable to Harlequin FASHION A WHOLE NEW YOU Offer. We will send you the specified gift.

OFFER CERTIFICATE

Item	A. ROMANTIC COLLECTOR'S DOLL (Suggested Retail Price $60.00)	B. CLASSIC PICTURE FRAME (Suggested Retail Price $25.00)
# of proofs-of-purchase	18	12
Postage and Handling	$3.50	$2.95
Check one	☐	☐

Name _____

Address _____

City _____ State _____ Zip _____

Mail this certificate, designated number of proofs-of-purchase and check or money order for postage and handling to: **Harlequin FASHION A WHOLE NEW YOU Gift Offer, P.O. Box 9057, Buffalo, NY 14269-9057.** Requests must be received by December 31, 1991.

ONE PROOF-OF-PURCHASE

4-FWHRP-2

To collect your fabulous free gift you must include the necessary number of proofs-of-purchase with a properly completed Offer Certificate.

© 1991 Harlequin Enterprises Limited

See previous page for details.